INFESTATION

WILLIAM MEIKLE

SEVERED PRESS
HOBART TASMANIA

INFESTATION

Copyright © 2017 William Meikle

WWW.SEVEREDPRESS.COM

ISBN: 978-1-925711-31-8

-1-

"This is bollocks, Sarge," Mac said. "Why are we jumping in the dark? We're out in the middle of nowhere; it's not like anybody's going to see us coming."

Captain John Banks smiled. Mac was always the first to complain; you could set your watch by it. It was a small bit of normality on a night where the normal was too far away. They cruised in darkness at fifteen thousand feet, somewhere to the west of Baffin Island, silent running through the Canadian skies. Twelve hours ago, Banks was ready for a spot of leave, even had a ticket booked on a flight to Greece with wife and both kids excited, packed, and raring to go. Instead, he'd driven them to the airport to see them off, before reporting to base at the urgent request of the colonel. Now where he was headed was going to be a tad colder. At least he had his own handpicked men with him, but it had been the only choice he'd been given.

"There's a Russian boat out there somewhere where she shouldn't be, John," the colonel had said back in Lossiemouth that afternoon. "And we think it's in trouble, maybe big trouble if the sketchy report we have is to be believed. There might be something worth salvaging though, and it'd be nice to know what they were doing snooping about so deep in Canadian waters. It's the usual deal for your team; get in quick, have a shufti, and report back. And don't get dead in the process."

So now Banks, his Sergeant Frank Hynd, and the small squad of four men he trusted more than anyone else in the world were out – in the middle of nowhere as Mac put it – getting ready to fall out of the sky into the cold black below.

All in all, I'd rather be in Greece.

"Coming up on drop point. Two minutes," the pilot said over the tannoy.

"Okay, Sarge," Banks said. "Line them up."

1

Mac looked like he might grumble again, but Frank Hynd put a stop to that quick enough – one look from the sarge was usually enough. The other three; McCally, Nolan, and Briggs – Tom, Dick, and Harry as the sarge called them – lined up behind Banks as the rear of the plane opened up, showing roaring blackness beyond. Mac and Hynd lumbered forward, shoving the box of their gear ahead of them. Banks counted them down from five and they rolled the box out into the night.

Seconds later, all six of them flew free in the air, following it down.

*

This was Banks' favorite part of any mission; the leap into the unknown, with butterflies in your belly and wind roaring all around you; it felt like freedom, even despite the bite of the cold and the frost forming at his lips and ears. In those early seconds, it scarcely felt like falling but more as if he skimmed, like a flat stone, across the rim of the world.

The rest of the men were merely darker shadows in the black but they'd done enough night jumps together to know they'd be in tight formation; and if any of them had a problem, it was too late for him to do much about it now.

He saw the chute of their gear box below him, counted to five, then pulled his own cord, following the other canopy down. It was a moonless night but also cloudless, the canopy of stars providing enough light for him to see the darker shadow of the island, their drop point, loom up below them. He looked over the shimmering waters of the bay to the north. If there was a Russian spy boat out there, it wasn't showing any lights.

But that doesn't mean they're not there.

He stayed almost on top of the gear chute all the way and came in for a perfectly controlled landing twenty yards to the north of the box. He had plenty of time to gather up his chute before the wind could catch it again and drag it away, then made quickly for the box; despite its weight, it was being dragged, albeit slowly, across the rocks, its passage facilitated by the ice underfoot. Hynd landed nearby and hurried to help. By the time they'd got the gear chute disengaged and rolled up, the rest of the team were gathered around the box. All save one and Banks knew who that must be even before he checked the faces.

"Where's Nolan?"

"I think I saw him drifting off west. You know Pat, sir," Mac said. "Fucking useless at this jumping lark. Could be anywhere by now."

Banks sighed.

"Okay, lads. Get kitted up before you freeze your balls off; five minutes, then we'll go and look for our lost lamb."

They were travelling light and fast so kitting up went smoothly; cold weather gear, lined and hooded parkas, balaclava hats, gloves and night vision glasses, each man with a flak jacket and webbing belt of ammo and a small backpack, a rifle and a knife. Banks knew they could all do a steady six miles an hour all night geared up in this terrain; he hoped to hell they didn't have to.

"Mac – you're on point, Briggs and McCally, you fetch Nolan's gear – the stupid wanker is going to be an iced lollipop by the time we get to him and it'll serve him right. Sarge – move them out."

*

The ground was icy but rough underfoot, slippage kept to a minimum by the deep ridges and treads of their boots. Banks warmed up almost immediately inside the parka but knew better than to unzip it; it was a clear night in late spring, but they were above the Arctic Circle and he couldn't afford to take any chances with the weather. He followed Mac as the Glaswegian led them quickly west toward where he said he'd last seen Nolan's chute. They were heading toward the sea; Banks could see it ahead of them, the shimmer clear in his night vision goggles. He could only hope that the Irishman's cack-handedness with a chute hadn't brought him down in the water, for if that was the case, he might be dead already.

Nolan was alive and blue with cold by the time they found him a few minutes' walk later, but he didn't seem to notice it; all his attention was on the scene around him. He'd landed on a rocky shoreline, yards from the water. His chute still lay, opened out and spread, behind him, soaked, looking black and glossy in the night glasses. Despite the lack of color, Banks knew from bitter experience what blood looked like in the goggles, and there was a lot of it on the chute.

Far too much.

Banks went straight to his man, fearing the worst.

"Nolan, are you hurt, man?"

Nolan didn't reply, even as Banks checked him out for a wound. But the blood wasn't the Irishman's and Bank's noticed it soon enough when he looked at their feet; they both waded in wet slush that was also running red, and when he followed Nolan's gaze along the shore, he quickly found the cause.

The beach had been home to a score or more of large basking mammals; walrus by the look of it given the size of the rib cages and the large ivory tusks he saw on the nearest body. They must have made an impressive sight hauled out on the shore, but now all of them were now little more than stripped carcasses. Gleaming bone and chunks of fat looked to be all that was left of the animals – that and the blood washing in and out with the small wavelets in the slush.

His team fell silent and still. Every man had his weapon in hand, and they'd taken position so that the squad as a whole had three-sixty warning of any attack.

"What the fuck, Sarge?" Mac said quietly.

Sergeant Hynd silenced the man with a finger to his lips and motioned that he would go south along the beach, sending Mac away to the north. Briggs and McCally got Nolan out of his chute and handed him his cold weather gear; Banks was glad to see that the Irishman was finally coming round from his shock.

"I missed the landing again, Cap," he said as he got himself into his lined parka. "I fucked up. Sorry."

Banks clapped the man on the back.

"Try to follow the rest of us. I've told you and told you, look below you, not at the view on the way down. You'll live longer. But at least you stayed out of the water. And you're still in one piece, that's the main thing, unlike these poor beasties."

Nolan's eyes were still wide as he looked around.

"What could do this, Cap? Polar bear?"

"Maybe," Banks replied, "if there were three or four of them. Maybe. Or, if they were closer to the water, I'm thinking a pod of orca might do this much damage."

But it didn't look like any kind of predator feeding Banks had ever seen. The carcasses looked like they'd been stripped and butchered rather than torn apart; it might be bears, but they'd have to be the tidiest bears he'd ever come across.

He put the thought away; whatever the cause of the carnage, it wasn't why they were here – he couldn't see how it had anything to do with their mission. Hynd and Mac returned from opposite ends of the small rocky beach.

"Anything?" Banks asked.

Hynd shook his head.

"Whatever did it, it was around this bit of the shore. And they must have left in the water. There's no tracks, no blood or spoor over to the south."

"Same the other way," Mac said and repeated his earlier observation. "What the fuck, Sarge?"

Hynd spoke dryly.

"I know one thing, Mac. It wasn't the fucking Russians; there's no empty vodka bottles."

Banks saw that the men were spooked by the extent of the slaughter around them; standing amid bloody ruin never did anybody any good, whether it was animal parts or human ones. He had to get the squad moving, before they all got the heebie-jeebies.

"Focus, lads," he said. "We're here for a boat full of Russian spies. If you see a polar bear, you have my permission to blow its nuts off, but we need to move and we need to move now. Nolan, you ready, son?"

The Irishman gave Banks the thumbs up.

"Okay, move out. Mac, you're still on point; Sarge, you watch our backs. If we dropped where we should have, there's an Inuit settlement two miles to the north; that's our first stop."

*

In the short briefing he'd had back at base before leaving, the colonel had told Banks they'd intercepted a garbled message from a remote settlement off Baffin Island, telling of a Russian boat in trouble in the bay to the north of them.

"The diplomatic boys have been on the phone all morning; we've asked for first crack at it and, subject to a few deal sweeteners to keep the politicos happy, you've got permission to go in for a look.

"We've got no idea how many Ruskies there are on board, or what degree of armaments they might or might not have, so sneaking up on them is the order of the day.

"The Canuck Air Force will be your backup," his superior said. "You've got twenty-four hours after the drop to get a report back here; if you don't, they'll send in the heavy mob."

It wasn't a particularly strange mission; Banks and the squad had worked similar jobs with tighter deadlines in worse conditions but the torn and bloody walrus remains had set a chill in his spine. His normally reliable hunch told him things might not be as straightforward as either the colonel had implied, or he had hoped.

The men were thinking much the same. They kept up a stream of low-voiced chat, all of it about the bloody mess they'd left behind them on the shore. Nolan, in particular, talked incessantly about the scene he'd landed in.

"I thought I'd crash landed, died, and gone to Hell," he said after describing his landing for the fourth time in as many minutes. "It was like a fecking horror film."

"Away and shite, ya big girl's blouse," McCally replied. "I've seen worse in Inverness on a Saturday night."

"Aye," Nolan replied deadpan. "Your mother always was a messy eater."

Briggs, McCally, and Nolan's laughter carried clear across the cold night, earning them an admonishment from the sarge.

"Keep it down, lads," Hynd said from their backs. "If the cap's right, we'll be coming up on the settlement soon."

That was enough to get quiet and they walked in silence for another half a mile. The terrain was easy going, hard-packed snow only occasionally punctuated with icy rocks they easily navigated and they made good time. Banks brought the others to a stop when Mac signaled from ten yards ahead of them; *trouble ahead.*

Banks left Nolan, McCally, and Briggs at the rear while he and Sergeant Hynd quickly moved up to Mac's position and joined him, lying flat on a frozen rocky outcrop, oblivious to the cold as they took in the scene below them.

An Inuit settlement sat around a sheltered bay at the foot of the slope below them – or rather, what was left of it sat there. The community had been made up of twenty or so buildings along the shoreline; six of those buildings were now little more than torn and shattered timber frames and many of the others showed signs of attack. Multiple smears, black in the night vision glasses but again all too obviously blood, showed on the track running along between the buildings and the water's edge. Two small fishing boats sat moored in the tiny harbor, one of which was listing badly, holed at the port side; the other was almost completely sunk, only the wheel house showing above the water. Out in the bay, several hundred yards offshore, a larger boat sat at anchor; it was too dark to see any identification and there were no lights on the vessel itself.

"Our Russian pals?" Hynd asked in a whisper.

"I guess so," Banks replied.

He turned his glasses up to full zoom and tried to make out more detail of the vessel but it was too far off in the night. He turned his attention to the harbor and checked the whole length of the settlement. There were no signs of any bodies.

But there's an awful lot of blood.

When Mac spoke, neither he, nor Hynd had an answer for him.

"What the fuck, Sarge?"

*

They took their time descending to the village, alert for any sound, any sign of attack, and taking care not to show themselves on the skyline. But no attack came. Nothing moved in the settlement below them save small wavelets lapping on the pebbled shore. The only sound was the crisp crunch of their feet on the snow and Mac's muttered curses when he slipped and almost fell.

Banks kept his eyes on the settlement, but the closer they got, the more obvious it was the people here had suffered a catastrophic attack to match the one visited on the walruses they'd found earlier.

A well-worn narrow path of small stones and gravel took them from the top of the ridge in a slow-winding meander all the way down to the waterline at the southern end of the bay.

The house at this bottom end of town had suffered less damage than some of the others had but when they walked off the slope and onto the shore-side track, they saw the main door of the property was smashed inward. It was as if a small car had gone straight through it, knocking the door in and splintering the timbers of the frame and surrounding porch. Blood smears, three of them, each a yard wide in the room before merging in the doorway, led from the house out across the path and into the sea, only stopping at the water's edge. A child's boot sat there, bobbing half in, half out of the slush, which was stained pink for six inches all around.

Banks, not wanting to ask his men to look at anything he wouldn't look at himself, stepped up onto the front porch of the house and approached the torn and shattered doorway.

"Hello?" he called out, then immediately felt stupid for doing so, as it was obvious there was no one home. The room was sprayed with blood, as if a mad artist had been at work with a pot of red paint, splashing it across walls, furniture, and carpets with abandonment. The power was out but Banks didn't need extra lights, he could see enough in his goggles. There were indeed no bodies here, just the blood and the smears but that alone was enough to tell him that no one had survived. Two of the blood streaks originated at a large leather sofa facing the television; the floor there was darker still and the sofa had been torn to shreds in places, as if by knives, or talons. The third lot of blood, which looked narrower than the other two, led from an overturned cot in the corner.

Their child's cot.

He could recreate the whole scene in his mind, apart from being able to picture what manner of beast might have been capable of this amount of bloody violence without leaving a trace of itself behind.

"Bloody neat bears," he muttered to himself as he went back

out to join his men.

Hynd and Mac were already investigating the next house up but it too had suffered the same fate. There was more evidence of a full frontal assault and smears, two this time, leading back to the water's edge, where some torn scraps of bloody clothing were all what remained of whoever had been dragged off. Hynd looked back at Banks and shook his head. He didn't have to say anything; there was no chance of finding anyone alive here either.

"Cap? What is this bollocks?" Nolan said and Banks heard the tremor in the man's voice. He'd seen Pat Nolan stand up alone to a frontal attack of a score of murderous mountain men in Afghanistan without a flinch, yet here he was, pale and trembling like a frightened boy.

"I know, lad," Banks said softly. "This is a bad one. But it's an animal attack of some kind, has to be." He patted Nolan's rifle. "Just point this at anything that shows up and fire until it goes away."

Nolan managed a wan smile as Hynd and Mac came back to join them.

"What the fuck's going on here?" Hynd asked but Banks didn't have an answer, beyond the obvious.

"First a Russian boat in trouble, then all out fucking carnage? I don't know. I thought at first the walruses were victims of a random animal attack. But I don't believe in coincidences. Eyes open, lads. This could be a rough ride."

*

The next two houses up the shore were much the same as the first; broken doors, no power, and bloody smears the only clues as to what might have happened. They found no signs of any weapons fire and although Banks checked the ground for tracks, looking in particular for Russian Army issue boots, he only found confusing scratches and scrapes, some almost bird-like, others more like gouges that might have been caused by claws. He had almost ruled out animal attack in favor of a Russian black-ops mission gone wrong but seeing those tracks, he wasn't so sure of himself again.

By the time they reached the fifth house, it was obvious the whole settlement had suffered much the same fate, although here there were signs of gunfire but from inside the house itself. The homeowner had a shotgun, a big one judging by the spray pattern of shot. But if he'd hit anything, there was no sign of any spilled blood other than his own. And this time, Banks got plenty of evidence to consider, although he still couldn't make sense of it.

The attackers hadn't dragged this victim away; the big man lay in the doorway, scraps of clothing and flesh scattered like a blanket under him. There was nothing left of his legs but bone and fatty tissue – *it likes its meat red* – his groin and belly gaped open, ribs splayed as if forcibly burst apart, guts and heart and lungs stripped as neatly as the muscles from the thighs, with almost surgical precision. All the attack had left him was his face, mouth gaping in a never-ending scream. Eyes, blood red, almost popped from their sockets.

Banks bent to examine the wounds more closely, wishing now he'd taken time to do so back with the walruses. The long bones of the thighs were scratched, scraped almost, as if the flesh had been scoured off roughly. And now he saw it clearly, he knew what it reminded him of – bodies he'd seen in the Himalayas, of priests left out in sky burials for the crows and vultures. The butchered body below him had much the same look to what was left; a scavenger had been at him, or rather, several scavengers.

"My local knowledge is admittedly sketchy, Cap," Hynd said softly, "but I don't remember any wildlife around here that attacks, or feeds, like that."

Banks stood, careful to avoid stepping in any gore. He shook his head.

"Me neither. But whatever it is, we can't spend time looking for it; we're on the clock here. Let's make for the Russian boat and see what's to be seen over there."

*

The small harbor at the center of town was as quiet as the rest of the settlement and neither of the two boats moored at the short quay were going anywhere except down; both were holed at the waterline, their timbers split, as if pulled open from the outside.

Banks looked over the dark stretch of water between them and the Russian boat. The distance could be swum, if they were in the Med; here it would be suicide, a certain death within minutes in the freezing water.

"Plan B," Banks said. "This is a fishing community; there'll be other boats or dinghies somewhere around here. We need to find one and we need to find one fast. Two teams; Sarge, you take McCally and Briggs and sweep 'round the backs of the buildings we passed; check sheds, backs of trucks, trailers – anywhere there might be a boat or inflatable. Nolan, you're with Mac and me. We meet up back here in twenty."

"And what if we don't find a boat?" Mac said.

Banks smiled grimly.

"Then we'll hollow out yon belly of yours and use you as a fucking canoe."

*

Banks moved quickly north with Nolan and Mac right behind him. The first building they investigated sat directly opposite the quay across the shore track; the local post office. Unlike the houses, it looked to have survived any attacks; Banks spotted it had concrete underpinnings and brick walls, along with a main door that was built to last; metal and glass at least half an inch thick. Whatever had attacked the settlement had obviously chosen the easier pickings to be had in the timber houses on either side.

He rapped hard on the locked door but everything was still and dark inside. Like the rest of the buildings, if there was power, it wasn't switched on. Either the locals hadn't thought to seek refuge there or, more probable given what they'd seen so far, the people hadn't been given the time. Whatever the case, a post office wasn't the right place to be looking for a boat.

They circled the building anyway, with Mac taking the lead this time. A small paved area at the rear had three Skidoos parked in a neat line. He made a mental note; the vehicles might be handy if they needed to make an overland getaway at some point... but as Banks had suspected, there were no signs of a boat.

Banks saw the other three men down to their south in the backyard of one of the houses; they didn't appear to be having much luck either. He led Nolan and Mac around to the front of the building to continue northward. Time was passing them by fast; if they didn't find transport across to the Russian vessel soon, he might have to call in an abort; a first for him and his squad and a step he wasn't ready to take.

"Step it up, lads," he said and jogged, almost ran to the next house up the shore. This one looked more promising, a larger property set back a bit from the shore with a double garage to one side that might, if they were lucky, prove to be a boat shed. But when they turned off the shore track onto the short driveway, Banks' hopes were dashed immediately; one of the garage doors had been pulled open and laid, a crumpled heap, to one side. There had been a boat inside, a fifteen-foot Zodiac dinghy. Like the boats in the harbor, this one was going nowhere; the rubber flayed, torn and tattered into ribbons with scraps of it laying over two more bodies; a woman and a child she had obviously been trying to protect. The woman's back was flayed open, her spine clearly showing. The girl below her had suffered less wounding, but her legs were similarly stripped clean of flesh, the bone showing too white in Banks' night vision. Nolan retched behind him and Banks turned to tell the lad to take it outside but never got to say it.

They all heard it at the same time, a scratching, scuttling noise, coming from the far corner on the other side of the dinghy. Mac and Nolan moved without having to be told, Mac circling 'round toward the far side of the boat while Nolan joined Banks in heading directly for the source of the sound.

The first thing Banks saw was a prone man's leg jerking as if in death throes.

We've got somebody alive here.

Then he stepped forward and saw what was feeding on the body and causing the leg to spasm.

*

Three of them; at first, Banks thought they were, surreally, armadillos, for they had the same armored look to them but these beasts were flatter, more oval in shape and definitely more crustacean than mammalian, with broad flat tails slapping on the garage floor as they fed. The more he looked the more they reminded him of the common woodlice that had infested his childhood home. But he wasn't going to be able to pinch these between thumb and forefinger; the beasts feeding on the dead man's guts in the corner were each almost two feet in length. They moved with great efficiency, the talon-like hooks on their feet tearing flesh in strips then fed it up along their length to an eager mouth that tore again, before passing into a maw. They chewed with sounds all too close to disgusting delight.

Banks saw Mac arrive on the far side of the body from him, weapon raised. He waved his finger – *no shooting* – he didn't want their presence here given away. But Nolan at Banks' side either didn't see the signal or was too caught up in his disgust to obey. He raised his rifle and put three rapid rounds into the body of the beast nearest him, the shots almost deafening in the confines of the garage. And as if it was a signal, all three of the creatures, even the one Nolan had so clearly hit, turned and as one launched directly at the Irishman.

*

Nolan danced backward, his weapon still raised, but the things were too fast for him and were at his ankles, clambering over his legs before he could move. He screamed as ribbons of material, then flesh, were torn from his shins.

"Stand back, Cap," Mac shouted and stepped forward. He kicked one of the beasts against the wall, where Banks was able to put it down; not easily, as it took three bursts – nine rounds – before it finally lay still. He turned to see Nolan trying to hold one of remaining two away from his face, even while its legs tore at his flak vest under his parka, trying to get at the soft parts.

Mac dispatched the second with three bursts of fire of his own, then both he and Banks were at Nolan's side, trying to tear the third off the Irishman. The beast flew into frenzy, legs tearing and ripping, Nolan screaming in terror, material flying in scraps of duck down and nylon. Finally, Banks and Mac got a clean grip on it, although Mac took a sliced cut across the back of his glove in the process.

"On three, into the corner," Banks shouted and on the count, they heaved the beast away from them. It immediately tried to come right back but by then all three men had their weapons up and ready. The creature blew apart in a deafening flurry of weapons fire, leaving behind only a smear on the wall and a ringing in Banks' ears that was going to take a long time to fade.

Blood streamed under the torn fragments of Nolan's trousers and the Irishman was pale, almost ashen but his voice was strong enough when he struggled to his feet and spoke.

"Going to need a hand here, Cap," he said.

"I've got dressings in my pack," Mac said but wasn't given time to do anything about it. More rapid fire carried in to them from outside.

"I'm right with you," Nolan said, all three of them left the garage at a run.

*

They only got as far as the shoreline track when they met the others running up from the south toward them.

"We need to find cover, Cap, and fast," Hynd said.

Over the man's left shoulder, Banks saw why; the shoreline heaved, as if the rocks themselves were alive, then they surged up and out of the water; the same kind of beasts they'd killed, scores of them, swarming up out of the slush.

"The post office," Banks shouted. "It's our only chance."

They retreated in the face of the rapidly advancing swarm.

- 2 -

Rika Svetlanova put down the box of hard biscuits and stood still, listening, sure she had heard something, far off.

An engine? Please let it be an engine.

But the noise wasn't repeated and she wasn't about to leave the safety of the pantry to investigate, despite the growing cold. She tugged her jacket tighter around her, thankful she'd been wearing her outdoor clothing when she'd needed to run. She'd been here for two days now going by her watch and had heard no other voices, had talked to no one. The power had run down on her phone hours ago, although there was little chance of getting any kind of signal down here almost in the center of the many layers of hull and metal. And she wasn't about to venture out of the room to look for company anytime soon.

It wasn't safe.

It might never be safe.

The boat rocked gently below her. As far as she knew, they were still at anchor in the bay, moored alongside the drilling rig; they certainly weren't under power, for she would feel the engines thrumming underfoot and hear the drumbeat thud of the turbines. Instead, all she felt was the gentle rocking, almost enough to send her to sleep.

Almost.

She had some light, so obviously an emergency battery somewhere was working but the bulb above her had dimmed considerably in recent hours. It wasn't going to be too long before she was left in darkness.

She'd been awake now for over forty-eight hours and had found herself dozing several times, snapping awake when her head nodded on her chest. But full sleep was going to be a long time coming and untroubled sleep a long time after that, for she had seen too much these past days to ever sleep soundly again.

Maybe I'll sleep when I get back to Moscow; my own bed, a good meal, and some large shots of vodka sound good right about now.

She laughed at the thought. Planning ahead wasn't a great idea, given her circumstances. She was in the main larder of the boat, with plenty to eat and drink at hand and a flow of air that, although it tasted of death at times, was breathable, for now. But to venture beyond the door might well be the death of her and she didn't know how long she'd stay brave enough to avoid opening it.

But she would go mad here if she stayed for much longer without doing anything.

If I cannot leave, at least I can make a report; it might be of use to someone, in the weeks to come.

She turned to her pocket Dictaphone, checked there was still power in the batteries, and spoke into it.

*

"I have decided to tell the tale here of our failure, in the hope that anyone who comes across this will not make the same mistakes we did, mistakes that have got us all killed... or worse.

"We got here in late spring. I know we're not supposed to be in Canadian waters but there's too much at stake here for us to ignore the wealth that's lying in our reach, opened up by the warmer waters of the Arctic. Someone will harvest the riches lying here, untapped as of yet. If we don't get it, another country will, and the Americans will be just as blind to the diplomatic niceties as we have to be. So we came across the Circle, determined to try.

"We went up and down the coast around here for several weeks, running seismic surveys, before deciding on the best spot for drilling. The week while the rig was put in place and made fit for operation proved to be a tedious one and I'm afraid I drank more vodka than was sensible and suffered for it with horrible hangovers and seasickness that had me quite debilitated for a time. But finally, it was done and we drilled.

"My job as chief scientist was to keep an eye on the sediments we brought up and check for value. As it turned out, I was kept busier than I would have hoped. The drill bit did its job for the most part, but the sediment, then rock, we drilled through varied wildly in porosity and density so we never knew from day to day how deep we would get, or what we might dredge up. I spent my days on the rig in the vicinity of the drill shaft trying to ensure the smoothest operation possible and my evenings in the mess with a never-ending procession of vodka shots and packs of Marlboro.

When I ran out of liquor, I took to getting beat by the captain at chess. The little Murmansk man was quiet but he had a mind like a steel trap and a game to match; I forced a couple of draws out of him but that was as far as I was able to get. We spoke little of matters beyond the game or the drilling, but he was a comfortable companion. I am going to miss him.

"In early May, we had a celebration when we struck an oil deposit and I'm afraid the lure of vodka got the better of me again. I staggered to my bunk and fell into a dark pit. I woke with a stinking headache, made all the worse by the loud ringing of an alarm and the incessant honking of our fog horn despite the fact bright sunlight lanced in through the porthole above my bunk.

"I went out onto the main deck and into a scene of almost comedic chaos.

"Stefan, the cook, stood at the gunwale, smacking something at his feet with a frying pan, again and again until whatever he was hitting was a streak of pulpy mush on the deck. Elsewhere, the crew stomped and yelled in a kind of macabre, badly choreographed, dance. It was only when I saw what the captain was holding at bay I realized this was no laughing matter.

"At first, I took them for horseshoe crabs; they were about the same, oval, dinner-plate size. But these had claws under the carapace, talons on their legs, pincers at the mouth parts, long antennae probing at the air as if tasting it and a squat, stubby rectangular tail rising in the air, giving them balance as they scuttled across the deck. I finally identified one as it stopped, raised its head, and tasted the air. I'd seen the like in books and on the Internet, but this was my first real-life encounter with the species. It was an isopod, *Bathynomus Giganteus,* normally a carnivorous bottom feeder.

"They weren't anywhere near the bottom now; the whole deck swarmed with scores of them. The one tasting the air turned on scuttling legs and came straight for me. I didn't think twice, I stepped forward and kicked it, hard, sending it soaring away over the gunwale.

"'I need some help here,' the captain shouted. He was at the main doorway into the superstructure, trying to close it against a frenzied attack of tens of the isopods. Three of the deck hands followed me in answering his call and we did what we could, stomping and kicking our way to his aid, leaving sticky trails of mush and slime behind us.

"The man next to me bent and tried to lift one of the things in his hands; it turned on him immediately, stripping two of his fingers to the bone with its rough mouth. Our stomping got more frenzied but even then the sheer number of the things threatened to overwhelm us. The noise of talons scratching on the steel deck sounded like tearing metal and the tap-tap of their legs as they scuttled was like rapid gunfire. Everywhere I turned there were more of them, and I finally saw the source; they came up the side of drill shaft and across the gangplanks from the rig, washing down in a wave onto the deck.

"My thought was we must have disturbed a colony on the seabed, enough for them to get curious… or hungry. It didn't bear thinking about.

"I kept kicking and stomping. Behind me one of the crewmen yelled in pain, bent to grab at where his ankle had been attacked and immediately had three of the things scuttling up his arms and over his body. I saw his left ear get ripped off, then he fell, immediately submerged in a threshing, squirming pile of the isopods, all eager to get to him and strip the flesh from his bones. His screams were terrible but thankfully, they did not last long.

"We had almost reached the captain at the superstructure door. He laid into the attacking isopods hard with a long tire-iron, cutting swathes through the beasts like a swinging sword. Between the four of us remaining, we cleared the doorway and were finally able to drag ourselves in and slam the door behind us with a resounding clang.

"We quickly made our way up the stairwell to the control room, where we all stood there, looking at each other for long seconds, each wondering what the hell had happened. The whole deck swarmed with the beasts, crawling and scuttling over each other in a frenzied search for food. I couldn't see any of the crew. I was hoping that, like us, most of them had made it to relative safety. At least the cargo hold doors were closed; I could only hope all remaining access points below decks were likewise firmly shut, for the thought of these things scurrying – feeding – in the corridors and cabins did not bear thinking about.

"'Now what?' one of the crew with us said. I realized the question had been directed at the captain.

"'Now we get these boogers off my bloody ship,' he said, his features set in grim determination. 'Brute force obviously works but let's try something a bit faster. Fetch the kerosene, we'll burn these bastards out.'"

*

"So began the longest day of my life. The captain dispatched crews all over the boat with only one remit – find any isopods aboard and get rid of them by any means necessary. As it turned out, fire was damned efficient, sending the things skittering away in search of respite from the flames. We were able to herd large numbers of them into an empty cargo hold where they burned, crisping and cracking like hastily cooked bacon. If I'd expected them to smell like a seafood gumbo, I was much mistaken, for the stench they gave off was acrid, like burnt vinegar, and they cooked down, not to the equivalent of shelled crabmeat but to a green, oily goop that smelled even worse.

"But our tactics were working.

"It was while I was helping to get ten more of the isopods into the dark hole of the cargo hold I saw the luminescence for the first time. It was only a faint blue shimmer, for there was bright sunlight coming in from the now open bay doors above dimming the effect. But now I'd seen it, I started to notice it in other dark corners where we found the beasts hiding. I knew immediately what I was seeing; the light they used to hunt by down in the depths was giving them away up here on the boat.

"As the day drew on and the sun moved 'round, casting deeper shadows in corridors and holds, I started to see the glow even stronger and along with it came a high, whining hum. I had to get up close to one of the things to find the cause; it rubbed its two largest limbs together, fast and furious and, like a cricket, sent out a message only its fellow isopods had a hope of understanding. But getting in close showed me something else and it was something needing further investigation. I didn't want to share the information with anyone just then but if I was correct, we were in more trouble than we thought.

"Much to the captain's disgust, I insisted on capturing a live specimen of the things for study; we finally caught one in a stout fishing net and I had it transported to the lab above the drill shaft out on the rig. I had no time to have a look at it then though, for the ship was far from clear of the things and it was several weary hours later before the captain pronounced himself satisfied.

"The last act of a long day was to go out onto the rig and pour a flow of kerosene over the rig and down the outside of the drill shaft then set it alight. I didn't hear any more of the high whine but I saw several small bodies fall, flaming, into the sea far beneath the main body of the drilling rig. As night fell, we scoured the boat for any luminescence but found none. The job was done.

"The captain set a guard on the rig just in case and I dragged myself wearily off to my bunk where I fell, fully clothed, into a welcome oblivion that did not require any vodka to achieve."

*

"Once again I was rudely woken, although this time it was still dark outside the porthole, and this time it was by the captain tugging at my shoulder.

"'We missed one,' he said as I rose.

"'It's alive?'

"'Not anymore,' he said. 'But there's something I need you to see and something we need to talk about.'

"He led me down to the main galley and through to the smaller, cold refrigerated larder at the rear. It looked like a gale had blown through it, with frozen meat, partially eaten by the look of it, strewn here, there, and everywhere. But it wasn't what he'd brought me to see. The remains of one of the isopods were squished into a mass of pulp on the floor, mere inches from its obvious entry point. A hole had been made, scratched or eaten, in the metal door of the larder, a hole the approximate width and height of the isopod itself.

"We left the cooks to clean up the mess and went up to the captain's cabin where, without asking, he poured us three fingers of vodka each and it went down the hatch so quickly I hadn't even got a smoke lit before he poured another.

"'Tell me again about the discontinuity,' he finally said after we were both lit up.

"We had talked, briefly, of the theory before, so I knew there was little he didn't already know but I also knew he needed to talk. The appearance of the isopods in such numbers and the loss of the crewman to them, had us all rattled. So I laid it out for him again as we made our way down the bottle. I spoke again of how our Russian scientists had discovered an anomalous layer between the mantle and the crust where sound waves behaved differently and the theories as to what might be the cause, from a porous rock stratum to large oil deposits or even, possibly, a liquid metal layer.

"At first, I thought he might not reply but then I noticed he'd definitely been thinking along lines I had not even considered myself.

"'These things, isopods you call them, you say they live on the bottom, on the sea bed?'

"I nodded, unsure where he was going.

"'But they only came up the shaft when we hit oil, when we broke through to a different layer. And here's what I'm thinking about, what if they came up from there and not the ocean floor? You saw how it ate through the metal door? What if that's what your discontinuity is? What if it's these things, down there, eating through rock and sediment and whatever the hell they can find? They're certainly voracious enough.'

"I was about to laugh, then saw he was deadly serious, so I took a long drag of smoke before replying, trying to compose an answer that would not sound condescending. I shook my head.

"'The pressures and temperature differentials would be too great at depth for any living creature to survive, let alone thrive in such large numbers. It's not possible –'

"He interrupted me.

"'And it's not possible for one of them to eat through a metal door. And yet here we are.' He didn't give me time to reply. 'And if they are bottom feeders we have disturbed, why didn't they come up when we started drilling and not this distance down below the sea bed?'

"His questions reminded me of something I'd forgot, the reason why I'd requested a live specimen.

"'I don't have any answers for you, yet. But maybe the one we caught will tell us something.'

"We made our way out onto the deck and across to the rig and the squat metal refurbished cargo container serving as my lab above the drill shaft. But our trip was wasted; the box lay half on and half off the shelf, clearly having been smashed open from the inside.

"'I think we've found where the one we missed came from,' the captain said dryly. 'Was there something in particular that caused you to collect it?'

I had hesitated to mention it until now but worry had suddenly taken root and I wanted, more than anything else, to head back to the vodka and dive into it but the captain wouldn't take my silence for an answer and insisted.

"'You're not going to like it,' I said.

"'I'm already bloody unhappy,' he replied. 'How much worse can it get?'

"'That's what I'm worried about,' I replied, keeping my voice low so only the captain might hear, for there were other men on the deck having a smoke and they were within hearing distance. 'I didn't get a really good look but I'm pretty certain the ones that came aboard today were all juveniles and all recently born.'

"'You're saying there are more?' he replied and I saw my worry reflected in his eyes. I hated to make it worse still but as captain, he deserved to be told.

"'I'm saying there are bigger.'"

- 3 -

Banks led the squad back to the post office, just in time, for the shoreline track, the short quay, and even the partially submerged boats were all now a seething, roiling mass of the scuttling creatures. The main door proved to be locked and it took both Mac and Hynd to force it open, having to break the lock in the process. The sturdiness of the door was a blessing in disguise, for when they got inside and closed it again, then manhandled a large filing cabinet against it, it appeared to be strong enough to withstand any attack, or at least give them plenty of warning of one.

Banks and Hynd stood at the main window overlooking the shore while behind them McCally and Briggs secured the main room and Mac worked on Nolan's wounds. Their night vision glasses gave them an all too clear view of the scene outside. Around a hundred of the beasts had gathered out there, all between the post office and the waterline, milling around, almost aimlessly. The only plus point appeared to be that they showed little interest in Banks' squad.

For now.

"What the fuck, Cap?" Sergeant Frank Hynd said, in perfect imitation of Mac's Glaswegian drawl.

"Fuck knows, Sarge," Banks replied in the same manner. "But at least we know what killed the walruses and the poor sods who lived here. I'll be buggered if I can figure out what it has to do with our mission though."

Now they saw the beasts in a cluster in the dark, something else was obvious; they gave off a shimmering luminescence from under their shells. Banks lifted up his glasses for a better look; as they milled around, it almost looked like they floated on a glowing blue carpet.

"What are they?" Hynd said. "I'd say slaters, but these fuckers are much too big. Some kind of crab?"

"Crustaceans of some kind, certainly," Banks replied. "And vicious wee buggers at that."

"We should call this in, Cap," Hynd said. "It isn't normal. We're way off script already and we haven't even got to the boat yet."

"You know the orders; radio silence they said, unless there's extenuating circumstances."

Hynd laughed and waved at the view beyond the window.

"I think this fucking qualifies, Cap. Don't you?"

Banks couldn't drag his gaze from the swarming beasts. He replaced his night glasses; the blue shimmering was too otherworldly, too far out of his experience. It didn't look quite so weird in the muted, almost monochrome world through the night vision. The beasts still showed no sign of being interested in them.

"We're not in any immediate danger, at least I don't think so. But we need to find a way past these fuckers; we need to get out to that boat."

"Well, I've got one bit of better news," Hynd replied. "We didn't find a boat or dinghy but we did find kayaks. There are eight of them neatly stacked behind the house two up from the south end, all in good nick from what I could see and all with paddles too."

Banks looked out beyond the beasts on the shore to the sea beyond. It was more slush than water and paddling through it in a kayak was going to be harder work than he'd like in this climate.

But it's better than swimming.

"Good work, Sarge," he said. "It appears we might have a plan after all."

"We've got to get past these things first though," Hynd said. "Any ideas?"

"I'm working on it," Banks replied and finally turned away from the window to where Mac had finished patching up Nolan's wounds.

"How's the patient?" Banks asked.

"He'll hurt like a bugger for a while but he'll live; it looked worse than it was. It's three deep cuts and a lot of scratches. He'll need a new pair of trousers though."

Banks addressed Nolan directly.

"How are you doing, lad? Can you put your weight on the wounds? Can you walk? We might be getting out of here in a hurry."

Nolan smiled and gave him a thumbs-up.

"Ready when you are, Cap," he said.

Mac tried to repair the gashes in the Irishman's trousers by binding the scraps of material with wrapped bandages. They looked too white in the night vision glasses, too vivid a reminder of the savagery of the beasts outside the door.

As Banks turned away, light flared up in his night vision like a bolt of lightning as the power in the post office came on, the lights overhead flaring, accompanied by a distant thrum.

"I've found the generator," McCally called from out back. "Let there be light."

"Shut that fucking thing off, right now," Hynd shouted but it was too late.

Banks removed his night vision glasses to allow his eyes to readjust and looked out to the shore. All the beasts had turned to move in their direction.

We've made them curious.

*

At least McCally had responded to Banks' order. The generator went off again and the lights dimmed, the post office falling silent, but the damage had already been done. The beasts came on fast, swarming around the area beyond the window. The main door rattled as pressure was put on it from outside and Nolan suddenly didn't look quite so happy.

Banks went back to night vision, then slapped a hand on the nearest wall.

"This place has concrete underpinnings and brick walls," he said. "They can't get in here; at least not easily. Keep calm, lads, we're safe, for the time being."

"How about the window, Cap?" Hynd said quietly, even as the creatures piled up against the wall, clambering over each other, the squirming mass already almost up to the level of the windowsill.

As they climbed and scrambled, the blue luminescence intensified, almost as bright as the office lights had been seconds earlier.

"They can't get in," Banks said again, but now he was remembering the broken and torn doorframes of the other houses; the big front window of the post office was in a wooden frame. It looked solid enough but if these creatures found a weak spot, he was pretty sure they wouldn't be slow to exploit it.

"McCally?" he said loudly. "Did you find anything useful out back while you were being a fucking idiot?"

"Just the generator. And a dozen twenty-liter containers of gasoline," the Scotsman replied, returning into the doorway leading to the rear of the building.

"That might be handy; lead with that next time, before using your initiative; it doesn't suit you."

The main door creaked, a loud squeal, as if the metal frame had buckled. Banks stepped across the room to the alcove where the door was and saw the beasts clawing and scratching at the frame where it met the ground. The metal was being shredded and taken apart, almost as easily as if it too was just timber. The door shook and moved slightly, the weight of the beasts' numbers pressing it open.

"We've got incoming," he shouted.

*

Another squeal ran through the night as the filing cabinet scraped on the floor; it had taken two men to move it into place but the creatures pushed it in as if it was an empty cardboard box.

"Little fuckers are strong," Hynd said as he came to Banks' side. They switched on the flashlights on their weapons and trained them at the door but the beasts took no notice of the light and kept pressing the filing cabinet inward, the sound of screeching metal wailing and echoing around them.

Banks was aware of the rest of the squad moving to join them; Mac at Hynd's side and the other three taking position behind them, ready to step forward when needed.

"Check those earplugs, lads. This is going to get noisy. Aim for the front end; if they've got brains of any kind, that's likely where they'll be hiding. Hitting the body hardly slows them down."

He pushed his own plugs in as deep as he could get them, then gave his full attention to the doorway. The filing cabinet squealed even louder, moved six inches inward, and the first of the creatures scuttled through an opening that didn't seem wide enough to accommodate it. Banks blew away the front of it, where he thought of as its head. It fell forward and went still. Two more scrambled over the top of it; Hynd put them down, the shots booming and echoing around them, deafening even despite the earplugs. Three more tried to come through and Banks was about to fire when he saw the ones behind had paused to feed on the fallen.

They're cannibals.

That immediately brought another thought and this one was a plan, of a kind.

He turned to McCally.

"Take Briggs and fetch as much of gasoline as you can carry," he shouted.

"What are you thinking, Cap?" Hynd shouted.

"A barbecue," he called back. "A bloody messy barbecue."

Then he had to shut up as the filing cabinet was pushed farther inward and half a dozen of the beasts filled the gap and came forward.

The air filled with the roar of rapid fire.

- 4 -

Svetlanova paused in her dictation; she'd heard the noise again and this time she recognized it for what it was: gunfire. It sounded too far away to be on board, too far away to be of any help to her and certainly not enough to shift her from her safe, for now, cubbyhole.

She knew she couldn't stay here forever.

But just a little bit longer. Please?

The overhead bulb had dimmed considerably now and she had to peer to see the stack of food and drink around her. Once the light had gone, she might be forced into having a look at what was outside the door. Then again, maybe she wouldn't, for her nerves were shot to pieces already; she wasn't sure how much excitement she'd be able to take before retreating into herself, to a quiet, safe place where things didn't skitter and tear in the dark. The cold bit at her but that she could handle; it had nothing on a Moscow winter.

She took the opportunity to arrange boxes and bottles so she would be able to identify them by touch should the bulb finally give out on her and plunge her into darkness.

More gunfire sounded, the rat-a-tat still too distant to be of help but she felt something stir in her that hadn't been there for a while. It felt like hope. But the feeling was short lived. As if in reply to the far-off sound, she heard something much closer; a scraping and scuttling outside the door of the pantry. She stood stock still, scarcely even breathing. She knew the isopods had no sense of smell as such but they had shown an almost preternatural ability to seek out food, especially fresh, or nearly fresh, meat. The light overhead was now so dim she saw blue flickering under the metal door.

It's right outside.

The scraping got louder and her panic rose, threatening to

engulf her, but when another burst of fresh gunfire roared in the distance, the scratching and scuttling moved off quickly.

Yes, go and investigate. Go, far away. There's nothing for you here.

She knew the truth of that as soon as she thought it. There was indeed little of any value to the isopods left on board, apart from the cold meat on her bones; she'd seen it for herself, in the headlong flight for safety that led her to this small patch of relative calm.

And I need to finish the tale; in case I don't make it.

She waited until she was sure the corridor outside was empty again, then returned to her dictation.

*

"The beginning of the end arrived four days and a few hours later, near midnight, on a moonless night and at first we scarcely noticed it. If it hadn't been for a slight tremor in the shaft, I might have ignored the initial signs completely.

"I'd gone to bed early but hadn't been able to sleep more than a few hours, couldn't bring myself to stay away from the drill rig for any great length of time. Drilling was proceeding smoothly and I only noticed the tremor as I was lighting a smoke. Despite a flat calm night, the match head trembled as I introduced it to the end of the cigarette. Then I felt it, the faintest of shakes underfoot but noticeably different from the normal slight sway brought about by the ocean swell. I thought the drill had maybe reached a different substrate and was struggling on a denser rock. I was even glad of the chance to get my hands dirty and do some work. I headed for the rig.

"One of the crew was up on the rig walkway above me and he let out a yelp of surprise as the whole thing shook, hard, and he almost lost his footing. At the same time, the drill shaft let out a loud creak as if it had come under some greater pressure from below. The drill revved, like a motorcycle being started, then leapt faster, still going down, yards at a time as if there was nothing beneath it to hold it back.

"My hands shook as I finally lit the smoke, this time it wasn't the tremor from below but sheer excitement and anticipation. We'd hit an unexpected void, or at least an area of viscosity that wasn't supposed to be there. Whatever was down there would already be on its way back up the drill shaft; and I was about to be the first to see what it was. I was only minutes away from seeing some results from all the hanging around in the cold. The shaking continued, less violently now than the first impact and the drill kept going, several meters a minute, an order of magnitude faster than before.

"The captain arrived having been roused from bed, still buttoning up his shirt and tucking it into his pants. He took a smoke when I offered.

"'Any minute now,' I said. 'We'll get to see whether it was all worth it.'

"By the time we had finished our smokes, the slurry was clearing from mud and rock to something much more liquid. An oily, rainbow sheen hung around the rig and the air tasted thick, almost greasy. I heard a rasp and a clatter, then the shaft coughed up a lump of something heavy, something the crewman had to drag out of the slurry channel with a tire iron. It fell to the rig's decking with a moist thud as the captain and I went in for a closer look. The oily sheen was much more pronounced now and it hung, shimmering in the air all around us.

"I don't quite know what I was expecting to see, mud and oil maybe, or sandy conglomerate. What I really didn't expect was to see a lump of tissue, and one most certainly alive, or at least had been until sometime recently and very recently – the beast from which it had come had obviously been right beneath the drill bit and been chewed up.

"What remained was all in one piece, about a foot across, the top part made of thicker, armored shell black in the gloom, with an underlying layer of what might have been muscular tissue, gray, almost white. The captain took the tire iron from Jose and prodded at the paler tissue. As the iron touched it, it gave off the blue, luminescent glow I remembered only too well. This was part of an isopod but one at least ten times the size of those we had previously encountered.

"'Captain,' I said softly. 'I think we might be in trouble again here.'

"The blue light shimmered in the captain's face, lending his aspect an almost evil glow, lit as it was from underneath, an old stage magicians trick, eerily effective here in the cold dark.

"The crewman on the rig shouted something, an incoherent yell I took for surprise. When I turned toward him, it was to see his face too was lit, blue and shimmering. But he was too far from the lump of tissue on the deck; something else was lighting him up, lighting him up from below his feet.

"I looked down through the grille of the iron deck of the rig. It was too dark to see the sea itself but not so dark I couldn't see the blue shimmering light, rising up from the depths, getting brighter, fast.

"I tugged at the captain's shoulder.

"'We need to get out of here,' I said.

"The captain looked down through the grille.

"'Is it those bloody isopods again?'

"I looked at the lump of tissue at our feet. The blue glow it gave off matched the hue and shimmer of whatever was coming up the side of the drill shaft.

"'Yes, it's them. But I think this might be something larger,' I replied.

"The blue rushed upward at a dizzying speed, the water at the surface roiled and boiled and an isopod the size of a small car came out of the deep and scuttled up the outside of the drill shaft.

"It came straight for us. We had little time to react but the captain made the most of it. Using the tire iron, he hacked, twice, at one of the kerosene drums until it split. The shimmer in the air of spilled fuel as a stream ran down through the grille and over the approaching beast. Even as we backed off, the captain was lighting a whole box of matches and as the scuttling isopod seemed certain to reach up toward us, he dropped the flaming box down the gap between the handrail and the deck. We leapt off the rig and down onto the deck as the kerosene went up with a whoosh, singeing my eyebrows and tightening the skin at my cheeks.

"But it did the job. We ran to the side in time to see the creature, already burning, fall away from the drilling shaft. It hit the sea, the splash rocking the rig and the ship moored alongside it.

The kerosene-fuelled flames hissed violently then it sank, the blue luminescence fading, slowly, into the distant dark.

"The captain turned toward me, a wide grin on his ash-blackened face. I was about to congratulate him when I saw the faintest hint of blue light again, lighting his cheeks and chin. I looked down over the gunwales.

"A large patch of the sea beneath the rig glowed, blue and silver and green, a pulsating shimmer like an aurora under the surface, rising fast. And this time, it was bigger still; it wasn't just beneath the rig. It was beneath the whole length of the boat, as if the whole bed of the bay where we had anchored was coming up to meet us.

"The blue came out of the water faster than I could make sense of what I was watching.

"The swarm came up and over the gunwales like a giant wave."

- 5 -

Banks stepped back to get a fresh mag from his webbing belt; Nolan stepped in front of him to take his place, never slacking the crack of rounds into the encroaching beasts. The creatures milled over and around each other in a growing pile of bodies in the doorway. Some kept coming forward but others were content to try to feast on their dead.

Banks got the new mag in and was about to step forward again when he felt a hand on his shoulder. It was McCally, with Briggs behind him; each man had brought two twenty-liter containers of gasoline through from the back room.

Banks looked back at the doorway; a slight incline led down to the door itself and then there was a steeper slope beyond the door as the ground went down to the shore track, a slope swarming with even larger numbers of the beasts.

The call has gone out; fresh meat available here.

"Fetch more of this shit," he shouted to the two men, then hefted the first of the containers, opened the cap and poured, emptying the full container. The gas flowed quickly away from him, pooling down around where the creatures swarmed around the filing cabinet in the doorway. The fumes smelled and tasted heady in the confined space.

"Cease fire. And back up," he shouted, getting out the old Zippo and a handkerchief from his pocket. "Fire in the hold."

He lit the handkerchief, dropped it in the gas and stood back, not quite fast enough, feeling the skin tighten at his brow, smelling the singe of his eyebrow hairs.

The creatures burned and popped, dancing like water on a hot griddle. Banks and his men had to step back even farther as an acrid stench of burnt flesh, almost vinegary, filled the hallway. The soft parts burned quickly and the beasts were reduced to little more than charred empty shells in seconds.

Well, you wanted a barbecue, didn't you?

They wouldn't need any more gasoline, or any more shooting; the beasts behind the burning ones in the doorway retreated in the face of the flames, backing off some yards away outside the door. The gasoline flamed away fast and within a minute there was nothing left in the doorway but a smoking mess of charred shell and burned fragments. Banks, with Hynd at his side, stepped forward and stamped down the remains into ash so they could get the door closed again, then pushed the charred filing cabinet back against it.

Hynd looked at him.

"Nasty wee fuckers, aren't they."

"Aye. Let's hope they're not too persistent to go with it."

Banks turned to the squad.

"Mac, you get first watch; keep an eye on these buggers. And if they look like they're coming back, give us a shout; we can open the door and pour a couple of canisters of gasoline down the slope; we might get a dozen or more of them."

Mac replied with a mock salute and Banks left the others back through to the main room. He was relieved to see the retreat of the beasts had been a general one; they had stopped flocking around the window and although their attention was still on the building, they were now keeping several yards back. If he thought they had any intelligence in them, he might surmise he had made them wary.

He turned to Hynd.

"We bought some time, Sarge," he said. "But we can't stay boxed in here; all they have to do is wait us out and we've got a mission, a boat to get to. Time's a wasting."

McCally spoke first.

"There's a wee yard out back, Cap," he said. "We could be out and away into the other yards in no time."

"I remember," Banks replied. "Skidoos too. But I'd rather leave them where they are in case we need to make a quick getaway later on. We'll slip out and head south on shank's pony."

"If they let us," Hynd replied but Banks ignored him and went to check out the yard.

The generator was housed in a storage area out back, looking over the yard where the Skidoos were parked. Banks opened the solid door, intending to survey a possible escape route for them. The next house south was only six feet away, but it might as well have been six miles. The yard was filling up with the creatures, scuttling and scurrying around from the front, already crawling over and around the Skidoos. The beasts saw Banks at the door and surged forward; he got it slammed in the face of the attack just in time and heard them throw themselves in frenzy against the heavy steel. This door was thicker than the one at the front; at least he hoped so, for he'd seen how easily they'd managed to tear strips out of metal.

"I've seen this movie," Hynd said, deadpan. "They're going to get in. They always get in."

Banks kicked at the stack of gasoline canisters at his feet.

"Aye. And if they do, we'll burn them back out again. I've seen this movie too."

*

The creatures continued to throw themselves against the metal door, the dull thuds echoing around the generator room.

Banks saw Hynd looking upward, then caught his gist.

"I've seen that movie too; hiding in the loft never works."

Hynd smiled.

"I was thinking more about the roof, Cap. Could we get over to the next building from there?"

Banks tried to picture the distance in his mind and nodded.

"It's a jump but if we can get a wee run at it, then aye, we could do it. But it doesn't get rid of the beasts."

This time, Hynd kicked the gas canisters.

"If we get enough of them in one place…"

Banks smiled grimly.

"A trap with us as the bait? Sounds like a cunning plan to me. See if you can find us an easy way up."

Banks went back through to the main room. Mac stood off to the right by the main doorway, keeping watch. Nolan and Briggs were by the main window, looking out over the shore where the creatures milled and swarmed.

"A routine mission... wasn't that what you said, Cap?" Nolan said. The Irishman was still pale but he looked little the worse for his earlier escapade. They both knew if they got out of this and got home, Banks would be having harsh words about the other man's break of protocol back in the garage earlier; but that was for later. Recriminations didn't get the job done.

Banks joined Nolan in looking out over the shore track. By his rough estimate, there were still more than a hundred of the beasts there.

And more round the back now too. Where are these fuckers coming from? And why now?

All he got for his ruminations were more questions he couldn't answer and none of which were getting the mission any closer to completion. But Hynd helped him out.

"Over here, Cap. Found it."

The sergeant shone the light on the end of his rifle up to the ceiling in the corner, to where a rope dangled from a hatchway. He pulled it, the hatch went up, and a step ladder came down. Hynd went up two steps and shone his light around in the space above.

"All clear," he said.

"Get ready to move fast," Banks said to the others. "We're taking the high road out of here."

Mac stayed on watch at the door while Banks got the others ferried up into the roof space; Hynd went all the way up first.

"There's a skylight window," he called down. "We can get out."

Banks had the men carry all but one of the gas containers up the ladder along with their packs, leaving behind only the one at Mac's feet. He called up to Hynd.

"Get everything onto the roof; then get yourselves out there. We're right behind you."

Only after making sure everyone was up and out did he call Mac over.

"You first," he said. As Mac put his foot on the ladder, they heard the front door squeal again as the filing cabinet scraped on the floor.

"Wee bastards have been watching us all along," Mac said.

"Aye. And I've been watching them."

Banks stepped forward and kicked over the gasoline, letting it gurgle all over the floor before following Mac up the ladder. He got to the top as the first of the beasts scuttled into the room. He pulled the ladder up behind him, flicked the Zippo into life, and dropped it down as he closed the hatch.

"Burn, fuckers," Mac said at his side.

*

The smell of acrid burning reached them even through the closed hatch and the floor under them got hot fast.

"Up you go," Banks said and helped hoist Mac out onto the roof, then allowed himself to be pulled up after him to join the others on the flat roof of the post office. Thin smoke rose up behind him; the fire downstairs had taken hold quickly.

"Whatever the plan is, Cap," Mac said, "we'd best get to it fast."

Hynd was over to the south, looking at the gap to the next building. Banks went and joined him at the edge of the roof. Fortunately, the next building also had a mostly flat roof and the jump didn't look daunting, little more than six, maybe seven feet.

"Mac and Nolan, pour half the gas down over the front door, Briggs and McCally, the rest down at the back at the yard door. And I hope somebody's got a match; I lost my lighter."

Hynd had matches, and a handkerchief he ripped in two.

"I've got a better idea than pouring, Cap," he said. "Molotov cocktails?"

*

They poured all but two of the gas canisters over the sides of the roof. By this time, smoke came through the shingles and heat rose up in waves at them; it wasn't going to be long before the roof itself took hold.

Banks slung his weapon over his shoulders to nestle beside his backpack, then sent everyone but Hynd and himself over to the adjoining building; Nolan almost didn't make it, his wounded legs giving way on landing but luckily Mac was there to steady him and keep him upright. The Irishman gave Banks two thumbs up when he recovered his balance.

"You ready?" Banks said to Hynd. They each held a container of gasoline with a gas-soaked handkerchief stuck in the open cap.

"Ready as I'll ever be," Hynd said.

"Is this going to work?" Banks asked as the sergeant lit up both containers.

"I've only ever did it with a milk bottle and petrol back in Cambuslang when I was a lad; I don't know about this Canadian stuff. I'll see you in Hell if it doesn't."

They each hurled the containers as far as they could out over the swarming creatures below, then ran for the edge of the roof and launched into the air as the gas went up with a blast of heat and flame behind them.

*

Banks landed hard but again, Mac was there to steady him. The weight on his back almost overbalanced both of them until Hynd steadied all three with an arm. They turned to see the post office fully aflame, the roof already starting to fall in on itself. In the yard at the back, the beasts burned. And they weren't going to get to use the Skidoos; the flames had taken them too and one of them went up with a dull *whump* as the heat got to the gas tank. The beasts not caught in the conflagration retreated fast toward the shoreline. None paid any attention to the men on the roof.

The main danger looked like it was going to come from the fire itself; the breeze off the sea whipped flames across the gap between the buildings. It was only a matter of time before this building went up along with the post office.

"Right, lads, time to go," Banks said. "Lead on, Sarge. Get us to those kayaks and get the flock out of here."

Hynd led the team quickly across the roof. They let themselves down easily on the far side, then, moving as one silent unit, headed away south into the dark.

None of the creatures followed them.

- 6 -

Svetlanova stood in almost pitch black darkness; the bulb above her was down to a single glowing red worm of filament and the only other light she had was the dim LED on her Dictaphone; she had no idea how long it might last.

There had been no more sound of shooting, not for a while now. She could only hope whoever it had been had survived and was now on their way to the boat; it might be her only chance of escape. And now that the darkness was closing in around her, she found she wanted to live, determined that this dark cell would not be the sum total of her life's ambitions.

She held the Dictaphone loosely in her hand; there was more yet to tell but she couldn't bring herself to speak it aloud; the memories came too raw, too vivid. The scant minutes after the wave of the swarm came over the bows of the boat would be etched in her mind forever.

The crew had died bloodily, some of them fighting, others pulled screaming from hiding places. Svetlanova and the captain had retreated into the lower decks via the closest access point to where they'd been standing at the instant of the attack, but they weren't given time to close the exterior door; the weight of the beasts was too much and they were too many. They were forced to retreat inside but the beasts kept coming. Soon, she was fleeing, full pelt through the corridors and down stairs with little regard for safety. At first, she was aware the captain ran right alongside her then one second he was there, the next he was gone. She turned, almost stumbled, to see the man get engulfed in a squirming wave of isopods, already tearing at the flesh of his legs and back. The captain looked her in the eye.

"Run!" he shouted, then was gone under as if drowning in the mass of tearing pincers and flaying hooks. She hadn't been trying to reach the large pantry; it was a coincidence the door was open when she reached it. She was planning to keep going, heading for the lifeboats at the stern but the corridor ahead was also blocked; three isopods engaged in dragging the flayed, thankfully dead, body of a crewman away.

She had leapt inside the open doorway, not really knowing where she was going, merely needing an escape, and slammed it shut. She'd stood there, fighting for a breath, her weight against the door, waiting to see if the defense would hold.

The beasts behind her had kept going. They sounded like a wave rushing along the narrow corridor. There had been more distant screams and several gunshots, then it had gone quiet. When her breathing recovered, she noticed she'd been fortunate enough to end up in the pantry. Something had settled in her, her mind determined a safe place was the best place and no other place would do.

The quiet had settled on the boat like a funeral shroud. Svetlanova could not risk calling out and if there was anyone else aboard still alive, in hiding like her, they too were being circumspect in their silence.

The boat belonged to the isopods now.

*

The first night had been bad. She ate too much; hard biscuits washed down with fizzy pop, far too much pop leaving her with an almost overpowering urge to urinate. And there was no way she was going to do it in the confines of the pantry. But the need was becoming far too great; an accident was imminent.

There hadn't been any noise for several hours, so she took a chance and pried the door open, a millimeter at a time until she had a clear view along the corridor, intending to retreat at the first sound, or first glimpse of shimmering blue. There was only darkness and deadly silence. The only light came from the room where she'd been hiding, the single bulb high in the pantry. The rest of the corridor was in deep shadows in both directions and she wasn't in any hurry to investigate the darkness. She stepped outside the pantry, some five feet along the corridor, lowered her clothes, squatted and did her business; it felt like much of her tension left her in the same moments and she found she was thinking straight for the first time since the beast's incursion.

She still wasn't in any mood for investigation though and stood, intending to step back into the pantry. That was when she'd seen it; a blue, shimmering glow right down at the far end of the long corridor running almost the length of the boat. Then she heard it too; the hum, high and whining as it communicated. Then it moved and she realized how far away the beast was; and how big it had to be for her to see it so clearly. It almost filled the corridor; five feet wide and the same again as tall; this wasn't one of the juveniles; this was a large one, like the one they'd burned and sent back to the deep. She'd been hoping there was only one of the larger ones but that was now dashed.

And where there's two, there can be many.

She had slid quietly back into the pantry and stayed still for many hours but nothing had come to investigate her presence.

Not yet.

Now all she could do was eat biscuits, ration her water, and worry, not about the infestation here on the boat but about the possibility of it spreading. Just how far the spread might go was a matter of speculation but everything she knew about isopods pointed in one direction; they liked to swarm and they liked to feed.

And they're not fussy eaters.

She listened, hoping to hear the gunfire again, hoping someone might be on the way with a rescue.

Hoping.

- 7 -

Off to the north, the sky was reddened with the flames from the still burning house and post office in the harbor, but the fire had spooked the beasts. For now, the yard where they stood was quiet and empty and they'd managed to negotiate a series of backyards to get here without any further encounters. Hynd led them into the dark shadows at the back of a squat timber house and removed the ties on a canvas sheet, drawing it back to reveal their proposed rides. The long slim vessels were raised up off the ground on a series of heavy timber railings to protect them from the ice and frost.

Banks stepped forward for a better look over the kayaks. The timbers they sat on were old, rotted in places but the kayaks themselves looked to be well maintained and probably seaworthy.

"I'm guessing they only take them out in summer," Hynd said quietly at his ear.

"Probably a great idea around here generally," Banks replied. "Unfortunately, we can't wait. Let's get these 'round the front to the shore. If the beasts are still concentrated up the other end near the fire, we might be able to slip off quietly out of the way. Best be quick about it, lads. The fire isn't going to burn forever and we've got a boat to catch before it buggers off without us."

The squad ferried the kayaks and paddles 'round the side of the house and down the short driveway to the shoreline, two men to each kayak, until they had six of them lined up at the waterline. Looking up the shore, Banks saw the beasts were still congregated a hundred yards or so to the north in the harbor area, near the now burnt-out, smoking ruin of the post office. He also noted something else – he wasn't going to need the night glasses much longer. The sky was lightening over in the east, a red tinge on the horizon showing dawn wasn't far off. When Banks took the night glasses off, the first thing he saw was Nolan's pale-faced gaze, studying the kayaks warily.

"I'm not going to enjoy this, Cap, me with the fucked legs and all..."

"Suck it up, lad," Hynd replied. "We're not leaving you here. Yon beasties have had a taste of you already. They would be having you for a light breakfast."

Banks waited until the rest of the squad got settled inside the long kayaks and slipped on the waterproofs at their waist to stop the freezing water sloshing inside onto their legs. One by one, he pushed them off the rocky shore into the water; he was the only one to get wet feet. To mitigate the cold, he had zipped the parka all the way up, pulling the hood tight over his head so the fur lining sheltered his face from the worst of the chill. He kept his weapon slung on the outside, hanging down at his chest so he'd only have to drop the paddle to reach it. His boots were laced up tight enough that the slushy water didn't penetrate but his feet felt like blocks of ice as he slid his legs into the kayak, although he felt almost warm after clipping the waterproof sheet around him. With the help of a pull from Sergeant Hynd, he got himself launched into the water to join the rest of the squad paddling in the shallows, holding their position, waiting orders.

*

The crab-like beasts had lost interest in them and the squad was able to paddle, albeit slowly in the slushy water, to a position some twenty yards offshore. The sky was much lighter already and all of the squad had stowed their night glasses. Pink washes above fiery orange lit the horizon and it might have been psychological but Banks felt warmer with the coming of the new day, even while bemoaning the fact they would now be in plain sight on their approach to the Russian boat.

Nolan looked paler than ever and a pained expression crossed his face with every paddle-stroke but he managed a wan smile as they all came together in a line.

"How you doing, lad?" Banks asked

"Guess the auld legs will do me for a few years more yet,

Cap," he said.

Banks turned to look at their destination. The Russian boat sat at anchor some quarter of a mile out in the bay; it was going to be hard work getting there in the slush, which was thicker in places and interspersed with larger blocks of ice to be navigated. The boat itself looked, at first glance, to be a typical cargo boat for these waters; a hundred meters or so long, with a high superstructure at the back end and a flat main deck with two large cranes to load and unload fish. What was different about this one was the attached drilling rig at the prow, taller even than the boat itself and looking solid enough, although even at a distance Banks saw scorch marks from a recent fire all across its surface. There were no lights on board and no sign of life on the deck or up in the superstructure. She looked dead in the water.

"Spy boat, my arse," Mac said and spat in the water. "They're fucking drilling."

"What do you think they're after, Cap?" Hynd said.

Banks shook his head.

"Oil maybe? Or gas? Could be anything. We won't know until we get there and we won't get there by sitting around here freezing our asses off. Keep your eyes peeled; any sign of trouble, anything at all, you know the drill. If some fucker starts shooting at us, take them out; don't bother waiting for an order."

They'd all been preoccupied with looking at the Russian boat and it wasn't until Mac turned and looked back to shore they saw something had changed; the harbor area lay quiet and empty; the beasts had slipped away with the dawn. The only movement was thin wisps of black smoke rising from the ruined burned-out buildings.

"What the fuck, Cap?" Mac asked.

Banks still didn't have an answer for him.

"Eyes front and rear," he said. "The fuckers could be anywhere and the boat's the mission here; we'll worry about the beasties when we have to. Move out."

*

The paddling was as strenuous as Banks feared it would be

and twice as cold. The early illusion of warmth inside the kayak proved to be a fleeting memory as an icy breeze coming across the surface of the water sucked all the heat out of him. His arms felt like iced-over wood, his arse like stone, and he couldn't feel his feet. But he kept paddling; it was better than the alternative. He also kept an eye on the boat ahead of them but the closer they got, the surer he was it was deserted, totally dead in the water. But it wasn't going to be easy getting aboard; he couldn't see any ladders or gangplanks to get them up onto the deck.

"Head for the drilling rig, lads," he said. "That's our best hope of getting up there."

As they closed in, Banks saw there were still two long lifeboats in their clamps at the rear of the boat. Whatever had happened to the crew, they hadn't abandoned ship by the conventional route.

We've got a regular Marie Celeste on our hands.

Mac went ahead to the drill structure while the rest hung back several yards. Banks took the opportunity to do a three-sixty check but it appeared the six of them were the only things moving on the bay. There were no birds; not in itself unusual in these northerly climes and no ripples disturbed the water. Even the wind, such as it had been, had died in the past few minutes, leaving everything flat and calm, the bay holding its breath, waiting.

But waiting for what?

Banks' spidey sense was tingling hard and he'd learned over the years to trust it.

"Mac?" he called out. "How's it looking? I'd like to get out of this thing before my balls drop off."

"Come on in, Cap," Mac called back. "There's been a fire right enough but the structure's sound and it looks like we can get all the way up to the deck, slick as shite off a shovel."

Mac led them forward into the shadow of the rig. It felt colder still here out of the morning sun, but they had ample room to quickly pull the kayaks out of the water and store them six feet up on the drill structure itself. It made extra work for them but Banks felt better knowing the vessels were there and safe, should a quiet, or quick, escape be needed without resorting to the lifeboats.

Five minutes later, they had the kayaks stowed safely on the second tier of the drilling rig and stood at the foot of a ladder leading all the way up to the deck.

"Time to go to work and find what we were sent to find, lads. McCally and Briggs, you're up first. Mac, bring up the rear. Heads up; and keep your eyes open. Quiet doesn't mean safe."

*

He felt every rung of the climb drain strength from his already weakened arms. On top of that, his gloves put too much of a distance between his fingers and the ladder, threatening to slip every time he tried to grip but he knew better than to go bare-handed; the cold metal would strip the skin from his palms as fast as any burn. Hynd was the man ahead of him and Banks concentrated on taking it one rung at a time, following the sarge's feet on the way up. The feeling he'd lost while paddling slowly came back in his feet and ankles, as if someone was running a blowtorch over them, and his breath froze into ice droplets around the fur of his hood. But he was doing better than Nolan below him, who moaned and complained every inch of the way up until Mac, below him, had heard enough.

"If you don't hurry the fuck up, I'll put a bullet in your arse myself, lad. Get a move on, I'm fucking freezing back here."

They kept climbing. It was only fifty rungs but Banks felt every one of them and by the time he clambered out onto the deck, his arms trembled and his shoulders ached from the weight they'd taken. At least it was warmer up here, marginally, and as he waited for Nolan and Mac to climb aboard, he raised his weapon, aware that now, this precise moment, was when they were at their most vulnerable. But the boat stayed quiet – more than that, it actually felt dead. Banks relaxed, as much as he could allow it, and had his first good look round.

Hynd, McCally, and Briggs also had their rifles in hand but there was no sign weapons would be needed; there was no sign, at first glance, of any disturbance. It was only when Banks looked more closely he saw it; more scorch marks, particularly around the top part of the drilling rig. Right on top of the rig, the metal was bent and twisted out of shape, as if something heavy had sat there once before being roughly torn away. Alongside that, there were numerous scratches and gouges on the deck; he'd seen their like before, on the shore where they'd found the dead walruses.

Our beastie pals have been here too.

There were no carcasses here though, no charred shells but as Banks walked several paces forward, he found the first clue as to the fate of the crew. A long smear of blood and tissue led across the deck and over the gunwales. It reminded him all too clearly of the similar smears they'd found back at the broken doors of the houses on the shoreline. There was something else too. The more he looked, the more he saw, deeper gouges and larger, longer scratches, far too big to have been made by any of the beasts they'd seen so far. It looked like only one set of them, but it had Banks thinking and he wasn't happy at his conclusion.

They come in bigger sizes.

*

Mac had to boost Nolan the last few feet up and over the gunwales; the Irishman had spent what little energy he had left on the climb but finally everyone was up on deck, rubbing their arms and stamping their feet to try to get some life into frozen limbs.

"Let's head inside," Banks said, "see if we can get a heat, or at least some respite from the chill. We'll try the control room first."

"Shall I take somebody with me down to check out the engines, Cap?" Hynd said.

"Negative. I want us all together until we know what's what. Last time I let any you off on your own, you brought back a load of hungry critters with you."

Hynd smiled.

"At least we got a fire out of it."

Banks turned to Nolan. The lad looked pale and dog tired.

"You still standing, Nolan? We'll see what's what inside, then get Mac to have another look at those wounds," he said and Nolan gave him the thumbs up but couldn't manage a smile.

"A cup of tea and a fag wouldn't go amiss either, Cap. I'm gasping and I've had enough of this running around shite for a while."

I think we all have.

Banks thought it but didn't say it.

"Mac, you're on point. We're headed into the superstructure and up to the control room. We'll take stock up there depending on what we find."

*

What they found was an empty boat. There were more blood smears; many of them, all leading across the decks or corridors and off the boat at the nearest vantage. What they didn't find were any bodies, although there was more blood in the first stairwell going up into the superstructure; the steps were sticky with it, despite it being congealed, almost dried. Whatever happened here, it had been a day to thirty-six hours ago by the look of it.

It was dim, almost dark, in the stairwell; the power appeared to be off and there was no thrum of engine or generator noise, only a gentle lap of waves on the hull and a slow, almost imperceptible roll in the swell. The only sound was the squad's footsteps on the stairs.

Banks looked up, past Mac to the top of the stairwell, checking for any signs of a possible ambush but there was only dark shadows, no hint of any of the blue shimmering luminescence he'd come to associate with the beasts.

He realized as they climbed he was now operating from the conclusion the creatures they'd encountered onshore were also responsible for what had happened here on the boat. He didn't believe in coincidence and certainly not one of this magnitude.

But what the fuck were these Russians doing here in the first place? And where did these beasts come from?

*

Banks' hopes of finding answers in the control room were dashed. Mac led them into a quiet, and most definitely empty, room; there weren't even any signs of an attack, no blood smears of gouges on the deck. It was as if all of the crew had suddenly left in a hurry; there was even a cold mug of coffee sitting by the main viewing window.

Hynd went over and checked the controls, then looked up and shook his head.

"There's no power. Either they switched it off, or something did it for them. We'll have to go downstairs to find out."

"Later," Banks said. "Nolan here had the right idea. We've been at it too long without a break. Smoke them if you've got them and we'll have a brew. Who's got the stove?"

Mac had the small camp stove and the makings for the tea in his backpack; they found a faucet in a small galley area off the control room and the water looked and smelled clean enough to drink. Banks was even able to get himself a mug of hot coffee by using a small French Press from one of the cupboards and helping himself from a jar of fresh ground Colombian. It was marked with a label, 'Captain only.'

That's good enough for me.

He made two mugs, strong and black, and took them over to where Hynd stood at the door, watching the stairwell. They kept their voices low; the other four were behind them in the center of the room, sitting on the floor, smoking and drinking tea, almost calm.

"What happened here, Cap?" Hynd asked, sipping at the coffee, then giving Banks a mock salute in gratitude.

Banks shook his head.

"Best guess? The beasties got in, overran them, and then left again. What the Russians – or the beasties – were doing here in the first place is the mystery. But I'm guessing it has got something to do with yon rig we climbed up on the way in."

"Any log book?"

"None I could see; I'm guessing it's all on the main computers. We need to get them up and running; that's the first job."

"We'll have to go downstairs. The main board for the generator is probably down there; and even then..." Hynd began.

"Aye, you said already; something might have been fucking with it. We'll have to go and check. And we're all going together. I'm taking no chances on this one; not when it's so fucking weird all 'round. And if we can't get the power on, I'll call for evac and let the suits back home sort this mess out. This is too fucking weird, even for us."

"Sounds like a plan to me," Hynd replied.

*

Banks gave the squad plenty of time to finish off their tea and have two smokes each but the day was already getting on. The shadow of the drill rig marked the sun's crossing of the sky by laying a dark, slow-moving patch of blackness across the deck outside the window.

"Okay, lads," he said. "On your feet. Time to get going."

Three of them rose but Nolan stayed where he was on the floor.

"Nolan?"

The Irishman looked up at Banks, fear in his eyes.

"Don't tell me, tell my legs, Cap," he said. "The fuckers have given up on me."

They got Nolan off the floor and up into the large captain's chair at the main control board. Mac sliced into the bandages, first removing the ones wrapped around the scraps of the Irishman's trousers, then starting on the ones dressing the wounds. All of them clearly saw what had been white cotton was now green, putrid, and giving off a stench that made them step back and breathe through their mouths.

Nolan's fear was clear in his eyes now.

"It's bad, isn't it?" he said.

Mac put a hand on the man's shoulder.

"We've got a mite cleaning up to do, that's all. This might hurt."

"I can't feel a thing below my waist, Mac," Nolan said. "Haven't been able to feel much of anything since I was sat in that fucking canoe. So you do what you need to do. Give me another smoke, could you?"

Banks watched as Mac cut away the dressings. The wounds gaped and the flesh on either side of the cuts had gone necrotic and blackened at the edges, oozing green, noxious fluid in their whole length. He'd never seen anything like it, nor smelled anything worse. The green goop looked to be foaming, as if boiling up from deeper in the muscle and sinew of Nolan's legs. Beyond immediate amputation, Banks couldn't see anything that would save the man. Mac turned, looked up at him, and shook his head. He had reached the same conclusion. It was beyond the man's experience to tend.

"Can you wiggle your toes, Pat?" Mac asked Nolan. He started putting fresh bandages on the Irishman's legs but as soon as he applied them, they soaked through with green.

Nolan laughed bitterly and took a deep drag on his cigarette before replying.

"I can't even wiggle my todger," he said. He looked up at Banks. "It's spreading, Cap, like I'm turning to ice from the feet up. It's a poison I'm guessing, a toxin on their claws? Take my advice, don't let the fuckers get close to you. But at least you won't get to put me on suspension for firing when I shouldn't have, so there's that to be thankful of."

"Don't you believe it, lad. You've got two weeks peeling spuds ahead of you."

Nolan laughed, then coughed and spluttered, pain crossing his face.

"Can I start now?" he said.

Banks was at a loss for a reply and Mac stepped in.

"Is there anything we can get you?" Mac said. All of them present knew what he meant; the chances of Nolan ever getting up out of the chair were slim.

"You lads go and do what you need to do," Nolan said. "Just leave me here with some smokes; I'll watch your back. Bring me back a fish supper and a bottle of Jameson's though, could you?"

*

They took turns in shaking Nolan's hand; Banks was last.

"Watch the door," he said. "And if it's not one of us, put it down hard and fast."

Nolan laughed, although both of them ignored the tears running down his cheeks.

"Hell, Cap," he said. "If you don't bring me a fish supper, I might shoot you on principle. Now get going. It's up to my waist now; when it hits my chest, I doubt I'll be breathing for long."

Banks shook the Irishman's hand. It felt as cold as the water he'd waded in earlier in the morning but Nolan managed to return his grip, then let go as Banks turned away. The last sight he had of Nolan was as he looked back on leaving the room; the Irishman had his rifle trained on the doorway and was lighting another smoke from the butt of the last. He gave Banks a salute and Banks saluted in return, before finally turning his back and heading for the stairwell to join the others.

- 8 -

She couldn't have told you how she knew it but somehow Svetlanova knew she was no longer alone on the boat. She hadn't heard anything but she'd felt it, a subtle shift in the air, a sense of life in a place where there had only been death. The feeling of a presence was quickly confirmed by the faint but unmistakable smell of cigarette smoke seeping in to her from somewhere in the boat.

She pondered whether it was worth taking the risk to investigate. Dim light came under the door; she knew from the clock in her Dictaphone it was morning.

And they mostly come at night. Mostly.

Suddenly, the thought of a cigarette was the biggest thing in her mind. Before arriving on the boat she'd only smoked two, maybe three a day but first boredom, then stress had got to her and her intake had become an addiction again all too quickly.

I am not getting myself killed because I need a smoke. I am not.

But she couldn't stay in the pantry forever, no matter how safe it made her feel. There had been no sign of any scuttling or shimmering blue, from outside for many hours. She was too much of a pessimist to believe the beasts had decided to go away, but she needed human contact to avoid going insane in here.

And I'm out of cigarettes.

She cracked open the door and peered along the corridor.

All was quiet and still, although once again she had the feeling she was no longer alone. The smell of cigarette smoke was stronger here too and the thought of having a cigarette and talking to other people was enough to give her courage she hadn't had until now. She stepped out of the pantry into the corridor and headed toward the smell of smoke.

*

The first room on her right was the main galley; empty and quiet now where it was normally a crash and clatter of pans and activity. There were no bodies, no sign of disturbance; it looked like the place was waiting for the crew to arrive and make breakfast. The mess, the next room down the corridor, was a different matter. Tables and chairs were overturned, crockery lay strewn and smashed on the floor and blood, far too much blood, splattered across every surface, arterial spray washing across the ceiling. Congealed blood and tissue had splashed the portholes, the dim light coming in from outside casting the whole scene in a red, hellish, tinge.

She backed away, even as she saw she'd been walking in streaks of gore. The floor was covered with it, the width of the doorway itself, showing where the dead had been dragged out, into the corridor and out of the door leading onto deck.

She headed in the other direction; she wasn't ready to show herself in the open just yet, feeling safer with walls around her. She moved quietly, not wanting to give away her presence and at the same time wanting to hear if there was indeed someone else moving around on board. She reached the stairwell leading up to the main superstructure. The smell of cigarette smoke was even stronger here. And as she stepped into the doorway, she heard something else; something completely unexpected. An Irish voice sang, high and pure, an old song Svetlanova had heard in bars and clubs in cities around the world; she had never expected to hear it here, on a boat she'd thought was long dead.

So fare thee well my own true love
When I return united we will be
It's not the leaving of Liverpool that grieves me
But my darling when I think of thee.

She followed the voice and the cigarette smoke as it led her up the stairwell.

*

So fare thee well my own true love. When I return united we will be

54

The singer started the chorus again but choked after the first line and a bout of coughing echoed down the stairwell, followed by a soft *'Fuck.'*

She had the source pinpointed now; the singer was in the control room. She went up the stairs quickly until she stood outside the door and decided discretion might be the best approach to introducing her presence.

"Hello?" she said loudly in English, guessing it was best after hearing the song and the cursing.

She got another cough in reply, then a weak voice answered.

"Either I'm already dead and gone to Heaven, or there's a woman at the door. Who's there?"

"Svetlanova, Chief Scientist," she said. "One of the crew of this boat."

"Well, come on in, then, Svetlanova, Chief Scientist, and let's be having a look at you. But be warned. I've got a gun pointed at the door and my nerves aren't at their best, so if you've got anything in your hands, best put it down now."

Svetlanova put her Dictaphone away in a pocket – she hadn't even been aware she was still clutching it until now – and stepped into the doorway with both hands raised.

A pale, ashen-faced man sat in the captain's chair. For her first few steps into the room, she only saw the gun, the black hole of the barrel pointing straight at her but after a few seconds, she guessed she wasn't about to get shot and her attention turned to the man himself. He was obviously ill, perhaps severely so. His eyes were dark and deep in his skull, a cold sweat ran at his brow and his lips looked dry, bloodless, almost gray.

He wore a heavy hooded garment on top but his legs were almost bare and as she stepped closer she saw why; a small pile of soiled bandages lay on the floor and green fluid oozed from deep wounds on the man's shin. She didn't have to think too long to know what must have happened to him.

He ran into the isopods. Or they ran into him.

"Who are you and why are you here?" she asked.

"I was about to say exactly the same to you, darling," he replied and tried to laugh but only a cough came out. He laid the weapon in his lap. Then he tried to light a cigarette but he lost control of his fingers and only succeeded in dropping his lighter on the floor.

"Bugger," he said and coughed again. There was an accompanying rumble deep in his chest, as if something wet was stirring inside him.

He's dying.

She stepped forward, trying to ignore the weapon, lifted the lighter, and lit his cigarette for him.

"You wouldn't happen to have another of those?" she asked.

"Inside my jacket here, top pocket, left side," he whispered. "You could give my nipple a wee tweak while you're at it; might be the last chance I get."

She found a blue and white pack of a brand she didn't recognize, *Embassy Regal* but when she lit it up, it tasted fine to her, not as strong as she as used to but better for it. The first draw went down smoothly and she felt the hit float in her head.

The Irishman smiled.

"I like a woman that likes to smoke."

They blew smoke at each other for a time. She sucked deep; because she enjoyed it and because it helped to mask the smell, almost acrid and rough on the throat, rising from the festering wounds on his legs. He saw her looking.

"Just my luck," he said. "I meet the only woman for a thousand miles and I've gone dead in the trouser department."

"What are you doing here?" she asked again.

He laughed, choked, and laughed again.

"Trying to find out what you were doing here. Her Majesty's government got curious and sent us."

"Special forces?"

"That's us. Just not quite so special at the moment; you're not catching me at my best." He coughed again and this time there was blood at his lips; blood and a hint of green.

"My captain will need to talk to you," he said.

"And I to him," she replied. "Where is he?"

"Engine room," the man said and coughed again, worse this time. Blood and green fluid bubbled at his lips. "Give him a kiss and say cheerio to him from me."

"What happened to you?"

"I got crabs," he replied, tried to laugh, then stopped when it forced him to cough up more blood and slime. "A really nasty dose. I'd stay away from the wee beasties if I were you. They're not friendly."

He dropped the stub of his cigarette on the floor. His eyes had gone cloudy, bloodshot streaks with green in them.

"At least I got to see a good-looking lass before the end," he said. "So thanks, darling."

And that was it for him. He died, between one breath and the next. Green fluid dribbled from his nose and mouth, the wounds on his legs foamed and bubbled and his chest sunk inward, falling in on itself. Svetlanova had to move fast; she grabbed the man's weapon and took it with her as she headed for the door. The stench rose in a wave threatening to overwhelm her. She had one last look back; the poor man's body looked to be melting, visibly shrinking away inside his clothing.

And I never even asked him his name.

- 9 -

The boat's main electrical panel was situated in a small room off the entrance to the engine room and Banks was grateful they didn't have to do too much stumbling around in the dark looking for it.

"We don't need, don't want, the whole boat lit up," he told Briggs and McCally. "Just get the power on to the control room. I need to get to what's on those computers. The sooner we do it, the sooner we can get off home."

There were signs of more death and carnage down here; scratches and gouges on the floors and walls, blood spatter and shit smears where the dead had been dragged off. Banks put on his night glasses, walked three steps out onto a gangway overlooking the main engine room, and surveyed the area.

It was no great surprise the power was out on the boat; the surprise was it was still afloat. Electrical cables had been pulled from their fittings. Neon strip lights had been tugged from the ceiling to hang below head height. A vast boiler had been overturned, holed as if torn open, and even the hull itself had been holed, near the water line at the far end of the huge, almost cavernous area. Water lay, a foot deep, all across the floor of the chamber and dim sunlight could be seen through torn and ripped metal, which looked to have been rent asunder in strips, as if it was little more than paper.

Hynd came to Banks' side. He whistled in amazement at the view.

"What did this, Cap? Iceberg?" he said.

"Aye, maybe, or maybe a big brother of one of those wee beasties?" Banks replied. "And if there is a big bugger around, I'm hoping he stays well away. The sooner we get off this boat, the happier I'll be."

"Do you think Nolan will make it?" Hynd asked. It was the first time any of them had spoken of it; it went against the grain to leave a man but they all knew the drill well enough: the mission came first. That was the first, the only law, they really had to adhere to, no matter how many corners they had to cut. But losing a man always hurt and Banks knew Nolan was lost; he'd seen it in the man's face, smelled it in the rot in his body. Hynd had seen it too; he wasn't really expecting an answer to his question and was talking to hear something, anything, in the deadly silence lying across the whole engine room. And again, Banks knew how the sarge felt; they'd been in empty places before – abandoned power stations, factories, and even whole towns. But they'd always felt dead and lifeless and none of those places had ever felt quite so alive, quite so threatening as this. He felt like a mouse circling a mousetrap, knowing there was something he needed, knowing there'd be dire consequences of taking it but needing to take it anyway.

And I know Hynd well enough to know he feels the same.

He turned to the other man and clapped him on the upper arm.

"Half an hour more, that's all. We get the power on to the computers, I get the gen, call it in, and we're offski, back into the kayaks and across to the pickup point."

Hynd didn't get a chance to reply. A loud splash sounded at the far end of the engine room, over near the tear in the hull. Both men turned to look as waves ran across the flooded floor but there was no other sign of movement.

*

Banks stepped back to where McCally and Briggs continued work on the electrical panel.

"Any joy, lads?"

"Maybe," Briggs replied. "Give us five minutes, Cap."

Another splash sounded somewhere out in the engine room; this one closer. More waves washed across the flooded room again but Banks still got no sight of anything else moving.

"Want Mac and I to take a closer look in there, Cap?" Hynd said.

Banks shook his head and stepped back to where the gallery walkway met the main corridor, a spot where he could see the whole length of the engine room and retreat quickly if he had to.

"Nope. Nobody's going to be doing anything stupid here; no wandering about in dark rooms, no splitting up – and definitely no shouting to see if anybody's there. If there's more of these beasties about, we leave them alone if they leave us alone. Agreed?"

Hynd nodded.

"Agreed."

"Nearly there, anyway, Cap," Briggs said. "Piece of piss."

A louder splash echoed through the engine room. Banks stepped back toward the gallery walkway and looked for the source of the sound. He didn't have to look far. One of the beasts stood between him and the rent in the hull.

This one was bigger – a lot bigger. As big as a family car.

*

At first, only the hard shell of its back showed above water. The dark oval suddenly scurried forward, sending more waves of water rippling through the flooded room. Then it came out of the water. It clambered up the inside of the hull opposite, so huge its head was nearly at Banks' level up on the gallery walkway before the rest of it was out of the water. He finally got a good, long look at it as it kept scurrying higher. The armored shell made it as well protected as any tank. Each leg looked longer than a man was tall and was tipped with talon-like hooks the length of Banks' hand and twice as thick. Two long antennae rose from the head, five, six feet long, each an inch and more thick and as rigid as any iron cable. They tasted and felt around the structure of the hull, as if deciding which part to eat. A wavering, faint blue luminescence hung all along its underbelly and he guessed it was ten feet, maybe twelve, from head to stubby tail.

He struggled with an almost overwhelming urge to lift his weapon and pour rounds into the thing but his own order echoed back at him in his head.

"We leave them alone if they leave us alone. Agreed?"

Agreed, he whispered and stepped back to the edge of the gallery. He saw Hynd look over his shoulder and reach instinctively for his weapon. He put a hand on the man's arm and shook his head but didn't speak, merely ushered Hynd and Mac backward until they were all at the door of the small room where the other two worked the panel.

"What the fuck, Cap?" Mac said, an exaggerated whisper that Banks put a stop to with a finger at his lips. Fortunately, everyone got the message. They stood still, barely breathing, as the thing splashed around in the engine room mere yards away from them. Banks was trying not to think – what if it could smell, or somehow, some other how sense their presence. What if it was even now squirting its poison in the air, what if they were all breathing it, what if...?

He forced himself to calm and motioned to McCally they should keep working on the electrical panel.

It's just a bug. A big bug, granted. But it's still just a bug.

He tried to believe it but hadn't quite got there yet.

Finally, Briggs gave him the thumbs up and he saw two small red LEDs winking on the control panel. He jerked his thump upward in reply.

Head on up.

He took the lead this time and left the engine room and up the stairs to head into the corridor beyond. He almost walked straight into a very surprised-looking woman holding a gun.

*

He didn't know which one of them was the more shocked but he had training, she did not, and he took the gun off her before she so much as twitched. He saw she was about to speak and maybe even yell so he did the only thing he could think of. He passed the spare weapon backward; someone took it from him but he didn't turn to see who, covered her mouth to silence her, and dragged her along the corridor, bundling her into the first room they came to, what looked like an engineer's cabin and bunk. His squad came in at his back and Hynd watched the door.

"This is Nolan's weapon," Mac said at his side. "How did you get it?"

The woman looked pale and wide-eyed but to her credit had quickly recovered her composure.

"He gave it to me," she said, her accent obvious. She avoided Mac, looking Banks in the eye. "He told me to come looking for you."

"Where is he?" Mac said, almost shouting until Banks put up a hand to stop him.

"He's right where you left him. Dying then, dead now," she said softly. "I was with him at the end."

Mac fell quiet and Banks saw the truth of it in the woman's eyes: Nolan hadn't gone easy.

And we left him to die alone.

He'd have to deal with it later, in the long-dead hours on dark nights. But for now, he had no time for guilt.

"You're Russian, right. One of the crew?"

"Chief Scientist Svetlanova," she replied. "And the only one left, I think."

"Well, Chief Scientist, I'd be grateful if you'd tell me what's going on here."

She reached slowly into a pocket and brought out a Dictaphone.

"It's all on here," she said. The sound of scurrying and scraping came down from somewhere above them and it was accompanied by a whining hum growing louder every second. "Do you want to hear it now, or should we maybe get somewhere safe first?"

*

Banks looked over to Hynd, who checked the corridor both ways, then pointed upward. The sound went up another notch, frantic scratching and scraping from many legs on metal decks.

"It's all above us, Cap, for now."

"And it sounds like it's more like the ones we saw in the harbor rather than the big fucker downstairs. Okay. Bugger the computers, we've got the chief scientist. It's time to go. Head for the stern. We'll take a lifeboat back to shore."

"We can't..." the woman started to say, before Banks turned to her again.

"Yes, we can," he said. "You're either coming with us, or

you're staying with them." He motioned upward with his thumb. "What's it to be?"

"But..."

Banks took the Dictaphone from her and stowed it inside his parka. He wasn't listening to her anymore; he had other pressing matters to deal with. The noise levels above them had become almost deafening; scratching and scraping, as if something was trying to get at them from above. Then he remembered the beasts at the door of the post office, tearing strips from the metal door and frame.

Maybe that's exactly what they're trying to do.

"You heard me," he said to the men. "Move out. Mac, you're on point. The lifeboats, fast as we can manage."

*

The corridor they were in ran almost the length of the vessel. Banks had a look up as they passed the stairwell to the control room.

I should check on Nolan. Just to be sure.

But he'd seen only truth in the woman's face when she spoke of the man's death. And besides, the noise was getting louder; wherever the beasts were, they were getting closer.

We'd be rats in a trap.

They went past a mess that looked like a bloody battle had taken place inside and a larder with an open door; the woman paused for a step there, then moved on in their midst, as if she'd come to a decision. They moved faster now as they approached the rear of the boat and finally the noise above faded into the distance behind them.

We're outrunning them.

They arrived at the stern seconds later, at the foot of another stairwell; if Banks' mind-map and calculations were right, the stairs would lead to an outside door and onto the small deck behind the superstructure where the lifeboats hung. Mac was already halfway up the first flight, the light from his rifle swinging wildly left to right as he checked his corners.

"All clear," he called down.

"Head up," Banks shouted. "And no glory boy heroics; we get in the boat and we fuck off out of here. Clear?"

"Clear," the men replied as one. The Russian woman looked like she wanted to talk again but Banks had already moved, starting up the stairs.

*

They came out, blinking, into too-bright daylight on a deserted rear deck. And Banks' heart immediately sank; yes, both lifeboats still hung in their cradles but there was a good reason they had not been used; they were both holed, the beasts had got to the boats first, the timbers torn apart from the inside out. The port side boat was in better shape than the other; the hole being only the size of a football. As Banks calculated the distance to shore and the time it would take to reach it, he knew even the small hole was too big; they'd be floundering in ice-cold water before the halfway mark.

"I thought this might have happened. I tried to tell you..." the Russian woman said.

"Try harder next time, lass," Mac replied.

Hynd had already moved to the port side and was looking along the length of the boat toward the drilling rig. He turned back to Banks and shook his head. Banks knew immediately what was meant.

The beasts are up on the deck. There's no way through.

They had two options – to head back down below decks or move upward on the outside stairs of the infrastructure. He wasted no time in coming to a decision.

"Move on up, Mac," he said. "I need to make a call and we need a clear, high spot for the best signal."

Mac led, the rest followed. The stairs led them round to the starboard side and as he climbed, Banks got a clear view of what Hynd must have seen from below. The beasts had returned and in numbers.

The swarm covered the whole forward deck. Most were the size of the ones they'd encountered in the harbor at the post office but up at the prow toward the drilling rig, there were others of much the same size as the one he'd seen in the engine room, ten, twelve feet or more in length. The huge ones fed on the smaller ones, even as they all milled around and over and under the legs of each other. As of yet, none of them were paying attention to the squad climbing up the superstructure stairs.

I hope to God it stays like that.

*

They reached the upper deck a minute later. The high vantage gave them an uninterrupted view of the bay, the burnt-out buildings in the harbor off to the south and the seething, teeming horde of scuttling beasts on the forward deck. Now they had the height to get a clear view, it was obvious where they were all coming from. The beasts thronged over and around the drilling rig, with one particularly large individual, bigger even than the one he'd seen in the engine room, sitting among the twisted metal right on top of the rig, master of all it surveyed. And still the beasts were content to mill around aimlessly, showing no interest in the squad up on the top of the superstructure.

"Keep an eye out, lads," Banks said. "One call home and then all we need to do is sit tight and wait for the cavalry."

He removed his satellite phone from deep in his parka, switched it on, and punched in the number. He had a bad moment when he thought the call wasn't going to connect, then it rang through.

"Cap," Hynd said and Banks heard a note of caution in the man's voice but the line had already been answered on the other end and he knew it would only take a matter of seconds. The sarge's concerns, whatever they were, would have to wait.

"We have a package in hand. Request uplift."

The reply was equally terse.

"One hour check in on this mark, four hours until uplift can be processed, coming down on your signal."

The call ended as abruptly as it had began but Hynd was now waving, almost frantically, for Banks to join him at the railing.

"Cap, you need to see this. I think we're in trouble."

They looked down; all of the beasts had turned so their front ends faced the superstructure and every single one of them had their head raised and antennae upright as the squad looked at the beasts and the beasts looked back.

"We got their attention," Hynd said, as the creatures, as if responding to an inaudible command, scuttled forward as one, heading for the superstructure.

"Time to go," Banks shouted. Mac was first to move. He went to the head of the stairs, looked down, and stopped in his tracks.

"Too late," he called back. "We're cut off this way."

"Take a quadrant," Banks called out and the four others each moved to take a side of the superstructure. "Don't fire until you have to. Short, controlled bursts."

He turned to the Russian woman. She was already on her knees, trying to turn the circular handle on a three-feet square hatch on the superstructure roof. Banks went to join her.

"We should be able to get down to the control room from here," she said. "But I doubt it's been opened for years; it's either locked or too stiff to open."

He bent to help.

"Here they come," Mac shouted.

Banks pushed his earplugs deep into his ears as the shooting started and the air filled with the crack and boom of rifle fire.

*

The hatch opening was stuck hard and even with the two of them pulling, it only moved an inch.

"Need a hand here," Banks shouted.

Mac shouted back.

"I'm a wee bit busy, Cap. I could use a hand myself."

Banks got his rifle in hand and went to Mac's side. He was still at the top of the stairs. The way they had come up was now a roiling, seething mass of the creatures, mostly the smaller ones, coming in a wave and falling backward on the steps almost as quickly as they climbed them. One, larger, horse-sized beast heaved itself slowly upward among the others and was only one level below Mac's feet. Banks remembered the feeding behavior they'd seen both at the post office and down on the deck.

"Get the big fucker," Banks shouted. "Give the rest of them

something to eat."

Mac saw his ploy straight away and between the two of them, they shot the whole front of the large beast's face away and it fell forward, blocking the passage of the smaller ones from behind. Those passed it immediately turned on it and started to rip it apart in frenzy as they ate.

"The more we put down, the more food they'll have," Banks shouted. "Slow them down as much as you can until we can get the bloody hatch open."

He went to check on the others. McCally had already moved away from his rail to help the others; there were no beasts on the southern side of the superstructure. Banks checked over the side, hoping for an escape route, but it was too far to drop down. If they had ropes, they might have chanced rappelling.

But if wishes were horses, we'd all be eating steak.

Apart from the stairs, the focus of the attack of the beasts came from the main forward deck. The rest of the squad stood at the rail overlooking the deck, firing downward to where a host of the creatures tried to clamber and climb over each other to reach them. Some were managing to get a grip on the structure itself and even with three guns, the squad struggled to stop the beasts reaching the top rail. Banks joined them and told them what he'd told Mac.

"Shoot the big buggers first; give the others something to eat."

They strafed the largest beasts within range, always aiming for the head.

"Shoot the antennae," the Russian woman shouted. "They're blind without them."

"You heard the lady," Banks called out. "Put these buggers down."

*

The downside of aiming for the larger of the beasts meant the small ones gained more of a foothold and several scurried quickly up the side of the superstructure. One reached the rail and tried to clamber over; Mac sent it back down with a punch to its belly.

"Don't touch them if you don't have to," Banks shouted.

"Remember what happened to Nolan."

He pulled Hynd aside.

"Give the lady a gun; we need more strength on the bloody hatch."

Hynd had Nolan's weapon slung over his back. He removed it and handed it over. The Russian took the weapon without a complaint, checked the mag, then stood at the rail next to Mac. Banks was glad to see she knew how to handle herself; it saved hassle he didn't need right then.

He bent beside Hynd and both of them put their weight into trying to turn the hatch wheel. It began to give with a screech, loud even above the noise of the gunfire.

McCally had to step back to reload; one of the beasts took the opportunity to scurry up and over the railing. Briggs put it down with a burst but he had taken his eye from the main body of them and two more scurried up to the top. The woman, Svetlanova, blew the head off the first and Mac took the second, by which time McCally had reloaded and rejoined the fray. But the beasts were now much nearer the top of the superstructure now and all four of the defenders had to step back as more came up to the rim of the rail.

"The antennae. Shoot the antennae," the woman shouted again.

The sound of gunfire rang and echoed all around as Banks and Hynd strained at the hatch opening.

"Put your back into it, Cap," Hynd shouted. "It's coming."

The wheel turned, slowly, too slowly; the beasts were now scurrying and clambering at the top rail and even the combined power of four rifles wouldn't keep them at bay for long. Parts of the beasts flew as the concentrated fire blew antennae, limbs, and shells to pieces and the roar of gunfire was deafening, even with the earplugs tight in Banks' ears.

But the wheel kept turning, even as the rest of the squad had to take another step back from the rail. All four of them stood in a line only a yard from the hatchway. Finally, the wheel gave all the way and Hynd was able to lift the hatch; just in time as the beasts poured over the rail in numbers.

"Back to me," Banks shouted. "Ladies first."

Hynd helped Svetlanova drop through the hatch, then all five of the men stood in the line, pumping rounds into the beasts, sending them dancing and capering on top of the rail as the bullets strafed them.

We can't keep this up for long. Time to go.

"McCally, you're up next. Get below."

The young Scot backed away, still firing until the last moment before he too dropped down the hatch.

"Sarge, you next. Make sure it's all clear below. We're right behind you."

The sergeant fired off a volley until his weapon went dry, then dropped away through the hatch. The three of them remaining were now sorely pressed to keep the beasts at bay.

"Briggs. You're up," Banks said but the man either didn't hear or was too involved in the battle to pay attention. He stepped, not backward but forward as one of the larger beasts came up to the rail with its antennae waving high above them, front limbs already reaching toward the men. Briggs was shouting now, incoherent cursing as he fired, not at the beast's head but directly into its belly. A blue shimmer rose up but the bullets did not affect the beast. It fell forward off the rail and its front talons raked across Briggs' chest, sliced and sliced again. The top half of the man's body came apart like ripped tissue paper.

"Get the fuck down the hole, Cap," Mac shouted. "That's an order."

As he was closer, by a step, Banks knew to hesitate might mean the death of both of them. He went down the hatch as fast as he could manage, falling more than stepping, six short steps down a ladder. Above him, Mac emptied his weapon and lunged into the hatch. Banks saw the Glaswegian reach to pull the hatch shut, saw a long limb cut, slice, across Mac's left arm, then the hatch slammed closed, the deafening clang echoing for seconds around them.

- 10 -

It had all happened so fast Svetlanova had barely had time to think. From the sudden death of the Irishman, meeting the British team outside the engine room, to the battle on the top of the superstructure and now, back in the control room, it had all happened in a blur of movement and a roar of sound and flying bullets. Now her ears rang, like church bells, too close, inside her skull and she wondered if she might not be permanently deaf.

The thinner man, Hynd the captain had called him, bundled her, first out of the small room below the hatch, then down a spiral staircase to the control room. He took one look at what was left of Nolan in the chair then wheeled the body, chair and all, through to the small scullery and closed the door on it. He couldn't disguise the mess on the floor; green goop, hardening, almost resinous, the last remains of the man she'd spoken to less than half an hour before.

Hynd took the hot rifle from her and said something but although she saw his mouth move, she couldn't hear a word, only the ringing in her ears, accompanied by a dull headache threatening to turn to pounding at any moment. She motioned with her hands at her ears.

"Deaf," she said, hearing only the faintest whisper of her own voice in her head but he got the message.

The rest of the men came down the stairwell into the control room. She saw them reload their weapons with magazines from their webbing belts but didn't hear the clunk as the new mags were rammed in place. There was only the constant ringing in her ears and no sign it was fading.

She needed to distract herself from her fear of deafness. She saw out the main window that the beasts had forgotten all about them again and were either milling aimlessly around the forward deck or feasting on the scraps and remains of their fallen.

What could have set them off?

She might have an inkling of an answer but the thought was driven away as she looked at the men; there was one missing, the stocky quiet one whose name she hadn't caught. And the others were ashen-faced and stern; she knew the look only too well.

They lost another man.

Then that thought too was dismissed; the last man down held his left arm in his right hand and dripped blood on the steps. The captain was already getting bandages from the wounded man's backpack. Svetlanova remembered the green slime running in the dead Irishman's wounds.

"Wait," she said and they all turned sharply; she'd spoken too loudly. "Don't bind the wounds yet," she said, trying to be quieter and headed for the scullery. She avoided the chair and the mess lying in it and went straight to the sink and the cupboard below it. She found what she wanted almost immediately and hurried back through to the control room.

"Bleach," she said, trying to keep her voice low. "Disinfectant." She heard her words stronger in her head now; her hearing might be coming back. The captain looked at her, then at the bottle in her hand and nodded; he'd got the message this time.

"This is going to hurt," she said to the wounded man – Mac, they'd called him – the one who'd called her 'lass' earlier. He put out his arm, rolling back the sleeve of his parka. The wound ran across the top of his wrist, white bone showing; he'd been lucky not to be cut any deeper; he'd either have lost the hand or bled out quickly. As it was, the wound gaped badly and bled profusely. They needed to get it bound up fast but she knew the pain the bleach was going to bring and hesitated to pour it.

"Just do it, lass," the man said and she heard him this time, as if he was speaking from the next room and behind a door. "Before I bleed all over you."

But I heard him.

She poured the bleach; and she heard his curses, then a long yell of pain clearly enough.

*

She took over nursing duties, closing the wound as much as she could with butterfly clips and binding it as tight as she dared with several layers of bandages. The man suffered it in stoic silence and smiled at her when it was done.

"Fine job, lass," he said. "Not bad for a Russian spy."

The captain took her off to one side.

"Thanks," he said. "He sat quieter for you than he would for one of us. Good idea with the bleach too. Will it be enough?"

Her hearing had got better. She heard the captain's question, only slightly muffled, although the bells still rang, albeit farther away in the distance now.

"I don't know," she replied. "It might be bacterial, or viral, or it might be a toxin. And the Irish boy may just have been unlucky to be caught by a sick beast. All we can do is wait. There's no way for us to tell without a lab; and mine was out there, on top of the drilling rig."

They both looked out; the large creature still sat there on top of the rig among the bent metal, like a resting cat, its stare equally as implacable.

"I need to know what you know about these beasts," the captain said. "And I need to know it fast."

"The isopods?"

"Is that what they are? Where did they come from?"

She still wasn't hearing quite right and rather than continue the conversation she tapped his pocket where he'd put the Dictaphone when he took it from her

"It's all on there. You should listen to it. Do you understand Russian?"

The captain nodded. The thin man, Hynd, checked Mac's wrist. So far, there was no blood, or green, seeping through the white. The Glaswegian flexed his hand and winced.

"Luckily, I wank with the other hand," he said, then looked up at Svetlanova and smiled. "Pardon my French, darling."

She smiled back.

"Call me darling again and you'll be scratching your arse with a stump," she replied, in her best Glaswegian accent.

Everyone except Mac laughed. He looked too surprised at first, then he too joined in.

"I like your new girlfriend, Cap. I think she's a keeper."

The captain was busy trying to figure out how to work the Dictaphone. She reached over and pressed the rewind button then, when there was a click, the play. Her own voice echoed back at her.

"I have decided to tell the tale here of our failure, in the hope that anyone who comes across this will not make the same mistakes we did, mistakes that have got us all killed...or worse."

She turned away – she didn't need to hear it. She looked out the window, only to see the beasts all looking straight at her. They weren't moving, weren't coming forward but their stares were unnerving. And yet again, Svetlanova had a feeling there was something she should be seeing, or remembering, something she needed to know. But as the bells continued to ring in her ears, so too did the thought elude her.

*

She took a smoke from the injured Mac when he offered one and smoked it down as the captain played back her statement, all the way through to the end.

"A large patch of the sea beneath the rig glowed, blue and silver and green, a pulsating shimmer like an aurora under the surface, one that was rising fast. And this time it was bigger still; much bigger.

"The swarm came up and over the gunwales like a giant wave."

She heard her last words, then a click as the Dictaphone turned off. She happened to be staring out the window at the time. The creatures had been still, staring at the window of the control room but as soon as the Dictaphone was turned off, they lost interest again and went back to their random milling and feeding.

The thought that had been eluding her was suddenly there, big in her mind.

They're reacting to electrical fields.

The captain put the Dictaphone down and turned to Hynd.

"I don't think we need them now but let's get these computers fired up anyway. Might as well take everything we can get while we're here."

"That's a very bad idea," Svetlanova said in reply.

Everyone turned to look at her. She quickly outlined her theory, finishing with her conclusions.

"They reacted violently when you turned on the satellite phone," she said.

The captain caught on first.

"And again to the Dictaphone, only less so?"

She nodded as he continued.

"And it would explain their behavior."

"It would?" Mac said. "I wish somebody would explain it to me, because I'm fucking lost here."

"At the post office, they didn't really come at us until we switched on the generator. And in the engine room; they've torn out all the electrical cabling and fittings completely. And they didn't come onto deck again until we buggered about with the control panel."

"You're saying we did it? We brought the fuckers back aboard?" Mac said.

"Afraid so," the captain replied. "But maybe we can get them to bugger off again by switching off what we switched on."

- 11 -

"Maybe we should stay here, Cap," Mac said. "We're safe here, right?"

Banks looked out the window to where the creatures continued to mill around, almost aimlessly. They hardly looked threatening now in sharp contrast to the frenzy they'd showed minutes earlier.

Maybe Mac's right. But twice now these buggers have caught me off guard. There won't be a third time.

"The chopper will be coming down on our signal," he said. "We need to make sure they have a clear pickup area."

"Back up on the top deck?"

"Not good enough; they'll prefer a bigger, more open space," he pointed out at the forward deck, "out there. Our best bet is to cut the power and hope the beasties, isopods, or whatever the fuck they are, get bored again and bugger off. McCally, can you cut the power from here?"

The younger man shook his head.

"That was Briggs' specialty. I'd need to get back down to yon control panel and see what's what. Although I'll tell you something for nothing, Cap; I'm pishing my breeks here at the thought of meeting one of those big fuckers down there."

"At least it'll keep you warm," Banks replied. "Come on, lad. You're with me. The rest of you, keep an eye out the window there. If they look like they're getting frisky, make plenty of noise and we'll get back sharpish."

Banks led the way out of the control room. It had got dimmer again in the stairwell, cloud obscuring the sun making it gloomy and gray away from the windows. He switched to night vision, turned down to its lowest level and was able to see clearly down the stairwell. There was no sign of any isopods. He gave McCally the all-clear sign and headed down, the younger man following at his back.

*

He stopped when they reached the corridor, almost exactly in the spot where he'd met the Russian woman earlier. She was still an enigma he hadn't cracked yet. He had a feeling there was more to her story he hadn't heard on the Dictaphone but he needed time to talk to her properly, time he couldn't spare right now. He had a feeling he'd need to sooner rather than later; she might have exactly the expert knowledge needed to get the squad safely out of the situation. It would all have to wait, for now. His focus had to be on the control panel and getting the infestation of creatures off the boat's deck.

One thing at a time, Banksy. One thing at a time.

At least Svetlanova had already proved her worth with her assessment of the effect of electrical field on the isopods. He was annoyed with himself that he hadn't seen the pattern in the beast's behavior for himself; it wasn't as if there weren't enough clues. But he'd been focussed on the job, which he'd thought was the boat's computers. As it turned out, the job, the woman, had come to him.

And now I've got a new job. I've got to get her back to the base; I've got to get us all back to the base.

He forced himself into concentrating on the space in front of his rifle barrel. The shock of losing Nolan and then Briggs, was still there, still thrumming at his nerve endings but his training kicked in, forcing the tension into something he could use, coiled and tight, ready to be sprung when needed. Later there would be recriminations, booze, and maybe even tears, certainly sleepless nights. But for now, he had a weapon in his hands, and there was an empty corridor and a waiting control panel on the deck below.

And if any of those fuckers get in my way, they'll find the real strength of my determination.

He moved out, quickly crossing the corridor to the next stairwell, then heading down toward the engine room with McCally right at his back.

*

The short stairwell to the control panel room was as empty as the one above had been. Banks stood there for several seconds, listening for any sound from the engine room beyond but there was no splashing, no indication the big beast was still there; for all he knew, it might be the one he'd seen up top of the superstructure.

The one who killed Briggs.

He pushed the thought away hard before thoughts of revenge could overtake common sense and motioned for McCally to come forward and get to work on the electrical panel.

McCally pried the front of the panel off and looked at the wiring.

"As I said, Cap, this was Brigg's party. I'm not sure what circuits he wired or shut off."

"Just do what you can, lad. And be quick about it. Sooner it's done, the sooner you get back upstairs for a cuppa and a fag."

He left the younger man to it and stepped forward into the doorway looking over the gallery walkway in the engine room. He didn't walk out onto the walkway itself but peered around the corner, making sure he was alone before announcing his presence.

There was no sign of the large beast but suddenly it was the least of his concerns; the water level in the flooded engine room was several feet higher than it had been. Judging by eddies and flows visible below him, more water was still coming in through the rent in the hull; flooding in.

The boat might be afloat now, but there was no guarantee it would stay that way for long.

He went back to join McCally.

"How long, lad?" he said, his voice a whisper.

"Depends. Do you want it off permanently, or just off now?"

"Just switch the fucker off," Banks said.

"Sorted then," McCally said and yanked at two wires. There was a flash, a spray of sparks around them, quickly dissipating. Everything fell quiet. The red LEDs denoting the power was on dimmed and went dark.

They both heard it coming at the same time; a click-clack and scratching of feet on metal, accompanied by a slosh of water as a wave washed through next door. The engine room wasn't empty anymore.

Banks put a finger to his lips and jerked his thumb upward. McCally nodded. The younger man stood closest to the exit, so Banks let him go first and waited while the McCally checked the stairwell up to the next deck.

He looked into the well to see McCally give him an 'OK' signal from above. Banks was about to step out into the stairwell when the scuttling suddenly got too loud at his back. He turned to see the head, antennae, and front legs of a huge beast push through the doorway. Its body was too large to fit in the doorway but it kept trying to get at the captain.

Banks tried to back away but misjudged the position of the doorway and got trapped in a corner. One of the beast's large antennae whipped through the room, as thick as a steel cable; it would snap his spine like a twig or cave in his chest if it hit him. He crouched tight in the corner, almost kneeling, giving a small target and finally got his weapon round to point it at the beast. The isopod chittered like a grasshopper and the blue luminescence on its underside sent out a shimmering aura, filling the small room with dancing shadows and the acrid smell of burnt vinegar.

Banks fought down a gag reflex, aimed for the base of the antenna, and fired three quick shots, the recoil shoving him farther back into the corner. The noise was far too loud and would surely alert any other isopods in the area to his position. But he'd got his target; the antenna hung, bent at the base oozing sickly green fluid, and the creature thrashed violently. The smell got worse too and splashes of the green goop washed the wall. Banks sidled to one side, ready to launch his body at the door if there was any chance of any splashes reaching him; he didn't want to get any nearer to the stuff than he had to.

"Stay down, Cap," a voice shouted above him and McCally came into the doorway. "I've got this one."

"This is for Briggs, ya bastard," he shouted and let off a volley, blowing the beast's face into flying scraps of carapace and soft parts. Banks had to shift to almost between McCally's legs to avoid being splattered in green. The blue shimmer on the underbelly faded and the beast let out an almost comical fart, then fell heavily on the deck with a thud before the weight of its now lifeless body pulled it back and off the gallery walkway out of their view. A loud splash echoed around them as it fell to the engine room floor.

A voice called out from somewhere above; Hynd had come down to the foot of the control room stairwell.

"You lads need any help down there?"

McCally called back up.

"Nah, the wanker's dead. It's sorted."

"Then get your arses up here, pronto," Hynd shouted back. "There's something you need to see."

*

Banks looked out the view window as soon as he got back to the control room; the forward deck was completely clear, the beasts gone as silently as they had come; even the top of the drill rig was clear of the large isopod they'd seen sitting there.

I hope it was you we got, you bastard.

"That's good, isn't it?" McCally said, but there was something else in Hynd's voice when he replied.

"The fact the beasties are gone? Aye, fucking great. But it's not what I wanted you to see."

He pointed north. A gray wall, an approaching storm front with paler cloud tops towering impossibly high above loomed over the horizon, getting visibly closer.

"Well, that's fucking marvelous, that is," McCally said.

"How long before it hits hard do you think?" Banks asked.

The Russian woman spoke first.

"An hour at most. We had one come through last week and things got a bit rough but she rode it out okay."

"Aye," Banks replied, "maybe. But I'm guessing she wasn't holed at the water line and shipping water back then."

"We could make for the kayaks?" Hynd said. "Head for shore?"

"We'd be sitting ducks if the beasts came for us," Banks replied. "Much as I hate to admit it, we might be better off here waiting for the chopper."

The rest of the words were unspoken but everyone knew they

were there.

Unless we sink first.

*

Nobody spoke for a while, watching the storm front edge ever closer. McCally left and went over to join Mac, making up a brew of tea on the stove and sharing smokes in silence. After a while, Banks checked his watch.

"Keep an eye out the window," he said. "I need to check in."

He took out the satellite phone, switched it on and punched the number.

"Check one," he said when it was answered and the voice at the other end replied in kind, "Check one." The line was immediately dropped but Banks was done speaking in any case. He knew there was no sense in giving any more update; none would be heard and the chopper was already on its way. He wasn't going to be able to get it here any faster.

He switched the phone off and looked to Hynd.

"Anything?"

"A big bugger poked its head up over by the drill rig but as soon as you switched the phone off, it fucked off again. We're still all clear."

"Well, it's something, anyway," Banks said, then looked out the window for himself. Several drops of sleety rain spattered like hard pellets against the glass.

The boat's hull creaked loudly and the vessel rolled several feet to port, then righted itself again. The storm clouds loomed to the north, a black wall getting ready to fall on them from a great height. The weather had already begun to ramp up.

Three more hours. That's all I ask. Just three more hours.

He wasn't sure they were going to get it.

- 12 -

Svetlanova had all of the men's names clear in her mind now. Her head too was clear, the ringing having faded into the far distance, her hearing almost back to normal, although she made a mental note not to stand so close to them if there was going to be more shooting.

She had also come to a decision on her immediate future; she'd thrown her lot in with these men, even when every fiber of her being was telling her to get back to the pantry and hide. She knew it was unrealistic; this team was her only chance of getting out of here. If it meant being taken to London for questioning, then so be it; Banks had already heard her recording and there really wasn't a lot more she could tell them they hadn't already heard or seen for themselves. In their vernacular, the Russians came, they drilled, they fucked up, story over. It made for a succinct, if short, report.

Over the last hour, she'd even developed a bond with the wounded Glaswegian man, Mac. She watched his wounds for any sign of green, all clear so far, and he gave her cigarettes and chat. They both thought they were getting a good deal.

He'd listened while she retold her story, having asked to hear it.

"Did you not hear when the captain played it back?" she asked.

"I'm Glaswegian, lass," he said. "We have enough trouble with English, never mind Russian."

It took a while in the telling, over strong sweet tea and more of Mac's cigarettes. He studied her with more respect after he heard the tale.

"How long were you in yon wee room?"

"Two days, I think."

"Then you're a braver man than me, lass. I'd have gone

mental."

"I'm not sure I didn't, for a while," she replied. She took another of his cigarettes. She was developing a taste for this British tobacco; and it kept her mind off what was going on outside the window.

The storm had already ramped up; beyond the glass was now a sheet of running water but she didn't have to see out to know it was bad. The rock and sway of the boat told her that, along with the now incessant creak and squeal of the hull sounding up from somewhere far below them.

Mac saw her apprehension and laughed.

"Don't worry, lass," he said. "These old boats can take a pounding. My auld dad built buggers like this on the Clyde and took me along to see them when I was a bairn; I know what their bones look like and they're hardy. And besides, this isn't even the worst scrape the cap's got us into and out of."

He started into a long involved story, of a brothel in Cairo, a girl who was really a boy, a misunderstanding about payment, and an epic bar fight followed by a hasty retreat involving half the Egyptian police force. The details of every twist and turn of the tale had them both laughing long before the end.

She was surprised to look up to see Banks take out the satellite phone for his next check-in.

*

"Is it worth the risk, Cap," McCally said. "You said yourself, the chopper's on its way already."

The captain motioned toward the window.

"If anything wants to come out in this weather to get at us, it's welcome to try," he said. He switched the phone on, checked in as before, and signed off again. If any of the isopods had taken note, it was impossible to tell. Hynd was by the door watching the stairwell and gave the thumbs up as Banks put the phone away.

"Two hours," he said. "All we have to do is sit tight."

"Can they land in this weather?" Svetlanova asked, for she knew from experience that nothing Russian would attempt to fly, never mind land, in the middle of an Arctic Circle storm like this.

Russian pilots were brave but they were also realists.

Mac answered first.

"Lass, the fly boys can land on a flea's arse in a howling gale. They'll be here."

McCally and Mac were now playing cards, three-card brag, with cigarettes as collateral. Svetlanova might have joined them, had Banks not taken her to one side by the window.

"You mentioned a discontinuity on your tape. You think it's where these things are coming from?"

"I'm sure of it."

"And what is it, this discontinuity?"

"An anomaly in the rock strata," she said, remembering what she'd told the ship's captain. "Ever since 1909 when Andrija Mohorovičić noted a zone where seismic waves speed up when they should be slowing down, people have been itching to drill and find out what's there. That's what we were doing here; our surveys showed us the discontinuity was closer to the seabed here than anywhere else in the world. Our geologists thought it might mark a huge gas field or, barring that, a mineral layer that could be cheaply mined."

"You're in Canadian waters," Banks said and Svetlanova waved her hand.

"The sea is the sea. Anyone can lay claim."

Banks laughed.

"I'm not sure the brass see it that way, but I'm not a politician. Tell me more. You pierced the discontinuity and these things came out of it? So effectively, you made a hole, sprung a leak somewhere down there, allowing the isopods out of their cage?"

"Yes, that's about the sum of it. We, as you say, fucked up. It's a big hole in the seabed. We put a camera down; I saw the footage not long before everything went wrong. It was in black and white of course, color cameras won't work at depth but even then the screen shimmered and glowed. The seabed looked like a scraped clean slab of stone, with tracks, almost like roadways, radiating out in all directions. There was a hole, glowing and gleaming like a flickering bulb, a giant eye, looking up at us from out of the earth's crust, daring us to poke it again.

"That wasn't even the worst of it. The hole had cracks

radiating out from it, the same radii, mirrored in the scraped tracks on the seabed, glowing tendrils pulsing and spreading even as we watched. Far from closing up, the hole down to the discontinuity was still growing. Isopods swarmed everywhere below. Big ones, small ones, a multitude of them, pouring up out of the discontinuity, scuttling and scurrying and quickly lost in the dark seas beyond the camera's reach."

"Why didn't you mention this before?"

"You didn't ask... and there's little we can do about it. The drill is kaput and unless you've got a submersible hidden in your jacket, there's no way down."

"Will they keep coming?"

"Given I don't know how many of them there are, whether they can survive for long out of their natural environment, or anything about their reproductive cycle, there's no way to tell. They could stay local to here..."

"Or they could spread," Banks finished for her.

"I've had plenty of time to think about it while I was stuck in the pantry. Imagine them getting into one of the main currents," she said. "The big one from here goes down toward the St. Lawrence seaway. They could get all the way down to the Great Lakes. Imagine them in Toronto, Montreal, or even Chicago. Imagine the carnage."

"Or going the other way, heading down the North Sea," Banks said. "To London. It's not a huge stretch to imagine one of those big buggers climbing Big Ben, or rampaging among the tourists in Trafalgar Square. We have to do something."

Svetlanova motioned to the window.

"We're on a holed boat, in a storm, with no operating drilling rig. You've lost two men already. What can we do?"

Mac looked up.

"I say we take off and nuke the site from orbit. It's the only way to be sure."

"Fucking A," McCally replied and the men all laughed as if they'd made a joke; she wasn't sure if Mac was serious or not but replied as if he was.

"That might work," she said.

Banks looked like he might reply but a gust of wind caught

the boat broadside and the vessel lurched, metal squealing. They rolled and Svetlanova lost her footing, tumbled into Banks and sent both of them to the floor in a tangle of arms and legs. For several breaths she thought they were going all the way over, then the old boat righted, almost over compensated, then rocked back into position. But something felt wrong now; they felt lazier in the water, too heavy but at the same time rocking and rolling more violently with the wind. Sleet, almost hail, spattered hard against the window.

Banks helped her to her feet and they looked at each other. Neither spoke, neither had to.

It's going to be a long two hours.

- 13 -

"We can't sit here, Cap," Mac said. "This crate's going down."

"Aye, eventually," Banks replied. "But I heard you earlier; these are hardy buggers and so are we. And we're not going anywhere in this weather. So sit tight and pucker up."

Banks couldn't bring himself to take his own advice; the thought of the flooded engine room was too big in his mind.

If the damage has gotten worse, I have to know.

Another thought was growing in his mind too. If the isopods were coming up the drill rig, then it probably wasn't a good idea to be so close to it. He had to find out whether they could uncouple from it, maybe even send the whole thing down to the seabed and how easy, or difficult, it was going to be.

Maybe the woman's idea of a massive strike is the right idea.

There was little he could do about the rig in the current weather conditions; he wasn't stupid enough to step outside in an Arctic gale if he didn't absolutely have to. But at least he could check the engine room.

"Watch my back, Sarge," he said to Hynd. "I'm going downstairs for a shufti."

"What about all that bollocks about not splitting up?"

Banks smiled.

"You can come and hold my hand if you'd like? I'm going to the foot of the stairs; a quick look at the engine room to check the damage and I'll be right back."

Hynd nodded.

"Okay. But I'll be down at the first deck level behind you, in case there's another of those big fuckers about."

"I think we're all clear; I think she was right about the electricity thing."

"I bloody well hope so."

*

Getting down the stairs proved quite an adventure in itself, for the roll and yaw of the boat had got much more pronounced since his last descent. He fell, hard, against the wall twice and was almost thrown off his feet when a gust of wind again shook the whole vessel. He heard a loud creaking, like tearing metal, from somewhere up near the prow.

Two more hours; give me two more hours.

The only good news in the engine room was that the hole at the far end didn't appear to be any larger. But the water was at least a foot deeper than the last time he'd looked, even accounting for the dead beast floating to and fro in the wavelets set in motion by the wind and the roll of the vessel. The wind howled and whistled through the hole and sleet, more like hail, spattered the hull like shotgun pellets. At least there was no sign of any more isopods and it didn't look like the big dead one had been scavenged in any way; with any luck, they'd be able to hide out the remaining time without worrying about an attack.

But the weather and the rising water level in the flooded room had him worried more than the thought of an attack. Mac had been right, the RAF lads could land a chopper almost anywhere, but the wind outside showed no sign of relenting. A rescue might not be as imminent as they hoped and the danger of sinking was rising with every passing minute.

*

"I don't think we can afford to sit and wait," he said when he got back to the control room. "This hulk might not last long enough in the storm."

"We can't take to the kayaks in this weather," Hynd said. "That would be suicide."

"Agreed," Banks replied. "But there might be another way to make use of this wind from the north. The shore won't come to us but maybe there's a way we can go to it."

He turned to Svetlanova.

"How are we attached to the rig? Is it part of this vessel?"

"You're thinking of floating away from it? We're anchored next to it and I think we're only attached to the rig itself by a series of cables. But I wasn't paying attention when it was put in place so I can't say for certain. And we can't lift the anchors without getting the main power on."

"I wasn't thinking about lifting them," Banks replied. "Mac, what are the chances of a boat this size not having an oxy-torch?"

"Slim to none, I'd say, Cap. Want me to go and find one? There'll be an engineer's stash around here somewhere."

"Just as long as it's not already underwater. How's the hand?"

"The lassie here's been looking after me fine," he said and blew Svetlanova a kiss. He flexed his fingers. "A wee bit stiff and sore and not up to punching anybody but it's not going to fall off, at least not anytime soon."

"McCally, you go with Mac," Banks said. "Don't do anything stupid. No heroics and no fucking about with anything electrical. Find me something to cut the anchor cables and get us away from that drilling rig. You've got fifteen minutes; then we'll be coming looking for you."

Svetlanova spoke up.

"I should go too. I know where the engineers worked, although I don't remember seeing a cutting torch. And I know where not to look, which should cut down the search time."

Banks didn't waste time arguing with her. He handed Nolan's rifle to her.

"I already know you can use this. Just don't get dead."

He addressed everyone in the room.

"Fifteen minutes then. We'll meet up at the prow, at the end of the long corridor where we came aboard.

"Move out."

- 14 -

Svetlanova led the two men toward the stern. She hadn't known the ship's engineers but she'd seen them around often enough to know where they worked. Instead of heading up into the superstructure, they needed to go down two decks at the rear of the boat. The crew's cabins were there and, below them, a large engineering workroom she had never visited but was where she thought they had the best chance of finding a cutting torch.

There was more evidence of the carnage that had befallen the crew in these darker corridors and room; men had been taken in their sleep or dragged out of closets in which they'd tried to hide. Blood splattered over walls, guts and fatty tissue lay in oily, drying smears on the floors and bloody handprints spoke of frenzied attempts to escape.

Svetlanova stopped, her toes touching a pool of congealed blood filling the corridor. The smell of death lay everywhere and somehow the sight of the carnage was worse here at the cabins, where crew were supposed to be at rest, supposed to be safe.

Mac put a hand on her shoulder.

"Eyes forward, lass," he said softly. "The only thing we can do for them now is remember them, mourn them, and revenge them if we get the chance. Your only job now is to get us to the engineering room; the sooner we get back up to cleaner air, the better it'll be for all of us."

She turned to him and saw the Glaswegian was favoring his injured arm, not using it for anything, just resting it on the top of his right forearm.

"Do I need to take another look?" she said.

"No time, lass," he replied. "We'll get it seen to once we get the job done here. It's fine."

His face told a different story; she saw pain etched there and more than a hint of worry.

But he's right. It won't matter much if we don't get out of here.

*

Her spirits lifted slightly when they descended out of the sleeping area to the next deck, but now they needed to use the lights on their weapons; whatever sunlight there was didn't penetrate down here and she found her bearings confused by the lack of artificial lighting. The rock and sway of the boat threatened to tumble her off her feet and down the stairs with every step. She let Mac and McCally go first while she directed from the rear.

"Two doors down is the one we want. There'll be a cutting torch there, if it's anywhere."

The two men moved more carefully now, focussed and cautious, weapons raised so they sighted along the light beams. Mac went first, waved is beam around in the room beyond, then turned and waved McCally forward.

Svetlanova followed them, five paces behind and alert to any sudden scuttling, into a large, dark room whispering with soft echoes as they made their way through it. The flashlights picked out workbenches, racks of power tools and parts.

"Bingo, ya fucking beauty," Mac said as his beam came to a halt on two tall cylinders in a wheeled iron frame. He went over, took hold of the pistol-like grip at the end of the cables, and checked the pressure valves.

"Braw. There's plenty of juice in these lassies. We've got our cutting gear."

His voice echoed in the empty corners of the room. In reply, a scurrying noise came from their left. Both soldiers had turned, weapons raised, before Svetlanova even thought to react. Their beams picked out a doorway, with its heavy steel door currently lying open. There was only darkness beyond, so deep their lights barely penetrated.

"What's through there, lass?" Mac asked.

She tried to picture the layout in her mind.

"There's a corridor running along the side of the engine room, then the main cargo bay," she said. "This must be an access door for the engineers."

The soldiers moved closer to the doors and she followed, peering over their shoulders. They looked down a long, empty corridor but she caught a glimpse of something that momentarily took her breath away – blue luminescent shimmering she knew only too well, in the distance, deep in the black shadows where the corridor became the cargo bay. Skittering, scratching echoed around the corridor, the sound coming from the far end where the blue shimmered.

"Close the door," she said softly. "Back away and close the door. Quick, before they notice us."

McCally moved quickly to comply and the door shut with a satisfyingly loud clunk. They stood still for several seconds but there was no noise now; the door ensured all sound stayed on the other side.

Let's hope it does the same for the beasts themselves.

"They're still on the boat," Mac said. "The fuckers are still here."

"I suspect they've been around for a while," Svetlanova said. She didn't voice her next thought; she didn't even want to be thinking it herself.

Scavengers never move far from a food source.

"We should be okay as long as we don't use any electricity," she said, whispering, trying to convince herself as much as the two men.

*

They stood, watching the door, waiting to see if an attack was coming but there was still only deep silence; they had evaded the beast's notice.

For now.

McCally checked his watch.

"We'd best get a move on," he said. "The cap will be waiting for this gear."

Mac went to move the iron rack and cylinders. He slung his rifle and tried to shift it with his good hand but the combined weight of the frame, cables, and cylinders proved to be too heavy for him. When he put both hands on the frame, it was obvious the pain would be too great for him to bear.

McCally had noticed too and stepped over to Mac's side, gently moving him away from the cutting gear. He arranged the cables, stowing them inside the iron frame between the cylinders, then rocked the whole lot back so all the weight was on the wheels. He pushed it back and forward a few feet, checking it rolled smoothly on the floor and nodded, seeming content he could handle it.

"You take point, Mac. We've got this between the two of us."

Svetlanova agreed, addressing Mac directly.

"I can take the weight on the stairs where needed. You watch out for us. Deal?

It was a sign of how much pain the Glaswegian must have felt that he went along with the plan almost meekly. They moved out again with Mac in front and McCally and Svetlanova piloting the awkward weight and bulk of the frame and cylinders along the corridor, following the dancing beam of Mac's flashlight.

The only corridor running the length of the boat down at this level appeared to be the one they'd closed the door on, the one with the beasts at the far end. To avoid it, they had to go back the way they came, to the stairs that nearly ended their journey when it had barely begun. Svetlanova and McCally heaved the rig up the first step; the weight of the tanks was almost too much for them and the frame's center of balance shifted as the boat rocked, threatening to topple it over on top of them. It took all of their effort and no little cursing on McCally's part, to stabilize everything.

It was slow work but they got into a rhythm of lifting and stabilizing, pausing at every step. Even then Mac had to use his good hand several times to keep them from all toppling back down the stairwell in a heap. That and the clangs and clanks of cylinders, frame and wheels banging against stairs and walls as the boat rolled and swayed under them meant it was two steps up and one step back more often than not. And all the while Svetlanova tried to concentrate on moving forward, while worrying what might be, even now, scurrying toward her in the darkness at her back.

Finally, they got up as far as the crew's quarters and as they moved, quicker now, along the corridor, Svetlanova's heart sank at the thought of yet another flight of stairs ahead of them. At least they had some light again, however dim, but the roll and sway of the boat was getting worse and the howl of the wind had gone up a notch, wailing like a banshee beyond the hull.

Mac was worse too; his face looked pale and etched with pain but he waved her away again when she offered to look at the wound. His accent was stronger than ever when he spoke, as if he didn't have the energy to moderate it for her benefit.

"Dinna fash yersel' lassie. I'm fine, or I will be when we get this bastard thing where the cap wants it."

"What does he hope to do with it in this weather?"

"It's his backup plan, in case the chopper has to abort," Mac replied. "He won't risk anything too dangerous unless he has to but he likes to have a plan for everything."

"I'd guess he didn't see this mess coming though, did he?"

Mac laughed.

"Don't underestimate the cap, lassie. When he wants to do something, it gets done and nowt gets in the way, either men with big guns, or your vicious, mindless beasties."

His gun slipped, and when he went to grab it with his wounded hand, he yelped in pain.

She reached for his arm to check on it but he pulled away brusquely. He was not quite fast enough to avoid her seeing the bandages. They had been white not too long before, but were now soaked, damp, not with blood but with watery fluid and more than a hint of green.

"We've got to see to this. And we've got to do it now," she said.

Mac had already started up the stairs.

"As soon as we get the rig to the captain; I've got my orders."

*

With more light at their disposal, the last set of stairs up to the long corridor proved easier to navigate, or maybe it only seemed that way now Svetlanova could see both in front and behind her and the fear of something rushing out of the dark had abated. But by the time they reached the top of the stairwell, Mac was clearly flagging and in great discomfort.

"It's gone cauld on me, lass. My arm is like a slab of iced-over iron and damned near as heavy. Have I really got what Pat had? Am I headed the same way? All those firefights and battles and close calls over the years and I get done in by a fucking poisonous bug?"

She had no good answer for him and he saw it in her eyes.

"I'm a soldier, lass," he said softly. "Something was going to get me one of these days. Let's get this rig to the cap and get the fuck off this boat. Hopefully you – or somebody – will get to see to me before I pop my clogs. But if not, I have no regrets."

I'll have plenty.

She didn't say it but she tried to move even faster as they pushed, pulled, and cajoled the cutting gear along the long corridor and the boat rocked and rolled and squealed beneath them.

- 15 -

Banks, with Hynd at his side, saw the others coming, headlong and fast, down the long corridor. Within a minute, all five were together at the prow exit leading up and out onto the forward deck.

Banks was already soaked through and frozen to the bone; he and Hynd had spent the last ten minutes out in the storm, checking out the anchor housings and the cabling connecting the vessel to the drilling rig. It hadn't taken them long to discover it was a larger job than they'd hoped. Clamps held some of the cables and some of those could be removed relatively easily once ice was chipped away from metal but others were corroded and fused in place; those were going to need cutting. With an oxy cutter on hand, it wouldn't be too much of a problem in better weather. But the storm showed no signs of abating; wind and sleet lashed a deck that rolled and heaved in a sea only getting heavier. It was going to be dangerous, almost deadly, work to disengage from the rig.

And then there were the anchor chains to deal with – two of them, inches thick black iron, both attached at spots wide open to the elements without a single hint of shelter. There was probably a place under decks where access could be had to the chain mechanism but it would involve more searching and working down there in the dark with the possibility of more of the isopods appealed even less than facing the weather.

Banks had hoped to get the job done in shifts, two two-man teams working in tandem at the cutting, giving the others some rest and respite. But one look at Mac put the idea to bed straight away.

"How you doing, Mac?"

"I've had better weekends, Cap. All in all, I'd rather be in Cairo."

Mac raised an arm to show the green-tinged bandages. The smell came almost immediately; rot and vinegar hitting hard in nostrils and at the back of the throat.

Banks spoke directly to Svetlanova.

"The bleach didn't work?"

"We don't know yet; it may have slowed the infection or toxin enough to let him fight it off. But he won't let me look at the wound."

"Hey, Cap, I'm right here," Mac said. "I don't have the energy to go out in the rain, I'll admit. But I can still watch your back and I can still handle a gun."

Banks spoke to the woman again.

"How about you? Can you work a cutting torch?"

She shook her head.

"I wouldn't know where to start. But I'll do anything I can to help. Just tell me."

"Do what you can for Mac," he said, then turned to the Glaswegian. "The nice lady is going to clean your bandages. Do me a favor, don't be an arse about it?"

Mac gave him a weak salute.

"You're the boss, Cap,"

Banks turned to McCally and Hynd.

"The three of us have got a lot of work to do. Zip up and gloves on. This is going to be brutal."

Hynd spoke up.

"You help with Mac. McCally and I will take first dibs," he said. "I'll send him back in, you join me, then we take it in turns?"

"Ten minutes max for McCally now, then I'm coming out and we'll rotate after that. We'll concentrate on the rig cables first; if we get lucky, the storm will take the rig apart for us. Then we work on the anchors. And if we don't get it done in an hour, it's not going to get done at all," Banks replied. "Move on out, Sarge. And good luck."

"There's something else, Cap," McCally said. "Yon beasties are definitely still aboard; we caught sight of them in the cargo hold but we let them be and they didn't bother us."

"Hopefully, the weather will keep them down below. But even if not, there's bugger all we can do about right now," Banks said. "We'll concentrate on the cutting and keep an eye open while we're at it; it's all we can do."

*

Banks held the deck door open while Hynd and McCally dragged the cutting rig up the short set of stairs. He let them out into the howl of the gale and spatter of sleet.

"Ten minutes, max," he shouted.

Hynd gave him a salute, then they were gone into the storm. Banks only closed the door after he lost sight of them; the sound of the wind abated in the corridor but not by much.

Svetlanova was already working on Mac. He sat on the floor, back to the wall, a freshly lit cigarette between his lips and a grimace of pain on his face as she unwound wet, green-tinged bandages. Banks went to take the soiled wrappings from her but she knocked his hand away.

"We shouldn't touch it if we don't have to. If it's bacterial or viral…"

He got the message and merely watched the pile of bandages grow on the floor. As they did so, the smell reached him even stronger than before, the same acrid stench that had come off Nolan. And Mac's wound looked to be in the same condition as the Irishman's. His wound had split the butterfly clips and was open, gaping and gray, with green goop bubbling and festering in the cut. Svetlanova started gently removing the seeping fluid with a cotton swab but more bubbled up as quickly as she wiped it away.

Mac looked at the wound and quickly looked away.

"Take the arm off, Cap. Find a big fucking blade and take it off at the elbow. I cannae feel a thing below my shoulder anyway. I'm up for it."

"Don't talk bollocks, man," Banks said. "The shock would kill you, if nothing else. Just hang on. The chopper's on its way."

Mac laughed.

"Now who's talking bollocks, Cap? We both ken they'll be avoiding this weather somewhere safe. Those fly boys might be full on fucking fuckwits and glory hunters but they're not daft."

Mac had voiced what Banks hadn't wanted to look at too closely, but he was right in his assessment. The chopper wouldn't risk it in this weather.

We're on our own until this storm blows itself out or the boat sinks. Either way, it's up to us to survive it.

Svetlanova had got the wound cleaned as much as she could and quickly finished bandaging up Mac's wrist with clean dressings. She lifted his chin to look in his eyes and in the process exposed his neck to view. Banks saw it but said nothing and turned away so Mac couldn't see his gaze; the big veins stood out proud, pulsing, not red but green.

He said a silent prayer to the weather gods.

Give us a break here. Mac needs help and I can't watch another man go like Nolan.

Mac looked up at him.

"Want a smoke, Cap? For auld time's sake?"

Banks laughed bitterly.

"Aye, that's all we need, another addict on the squad. You have one for me. I'll stick with the whisky and have two with you back in the mess when we get home."

Mac didn't reply.

He knows a lie when he hears one.

Mac and Svetlanova smoked in silence for a time and McCally returned not long after Mac finished his cigarette. The door opened, letting in a wash of sleet and a howl of wind, then he stepped in and shut it behind him quickly.

"How's it going?" Banks asked as McCally shook off icy sleet from his jacket and legs.

"The clamps are undone and two of the four cables holding the rig," he said. He had more ice at chin and nose, his eyebrows looked frozen to his forehead, and he was soaked through. He looked about as miserable as anyone Banks had ever seen.

And now it's my turn.

"Get out of the jacket at least," he said as he made for the door. "Wear Mac's the next time out. It'll help."

He saw the look on McCally's face; it wouldn't be helping much.

He pulled his jacket as tight around him as he could manage, pulled his hood around his face until he only had a small viewing area ahead of him, left his weapon on the floor at Mac's side, and headed out into the storm.

*

Wind and sleet hit him face on almost immediately. He turned sideward into it, got his bearings on where the drilling rig would be some ten yards to his right and, bent almost double, headed toward it.

After two steps that felt like twenty, fighting the gale for every inch, he saw the blue flare of the cutting torch and was able to follow the light to where he found Hynd, hunched over one of the drilling rig cables.

"Last one, Cap," Hynd shouted, his voice almost completely lost in the wind. The cable parted and, not bothering to switch the torch off, Hynd and Banks dragged the iron frame and the cylinders across the deck towards the first of the anchor chains.

The weight and heft of the frame was enough to give them some stability but as soon as they got to the first anchor cable, the wind threatened to tug them, tools, canisters and men, off to one side and it was a constant fight against it. They used the canisters themselves as a makeshift windbreak, with Banks keeping them upright with his back against the frame while Hynd worked. He turned the flame yellow and started the long process of warming the anchor chain enough so it might be able to be cut. The wind lashed at them, sleet hammered against their hoods and backs and legs and Hynd struggled to keep the flame on the same piece of chain for more than a few seconds at a time.

This is going to take a while. And it's a while we don't have.

Banks checked the gauges; they'd used up almost half of their oxygen already and still had the bulk of the cutting to do.

- 16 -

Svetlanova listened while Mac talked and McCally tried to get some warmth into his hands and feet. They all smoked Mac's cigarettes and the Glaswegian was getting maudlin.

"I want you to go and say goodbye to my auld maw, McCally. She likes you. Hell, she likes you more than she likes me I think. But she's my maw and she should ken I was thinking of her, at the end."

"The end? Don't talk pish, man," McCally replied. "You can tell her yourself when we get back."

Mac lowered his hood and showed McCally his neck.

"You all didn't think I'd noticed, did you. But I can feel it, like ice in my veins. It's fucking freezing. It's creeping up towards my ear now. When it gets to my brain, I'm guessing that's it for me."

McCally tried for a laugh.

"Away and shite, man," he said. "You've managed without any brains for fucking years, you'll survive a while longer yet."

He never got a reply, for the door slammed open and Hynd came back in. He looked even colder and wetter than McCally had earlier, something Svetlanova wouldn't have thought possible.

"We're on the first anchor chain, the one on the starboard side. You're up, McCally," he said through lips that almost looked frozen.

"Do you want my jacket?" Mac said and started to take is parka off, only to reveal a smear of green inside the sleeve, which was damp all the way up to the elbow.

"You're okay, big man," McCally said. "I'll pass this time. Maybe next go-round, eh?"

McCally left and Hynd closed the door behind him then staggered, almost fell. Svetlanova didn't stop to think. She unzipped the man's jacket, shucked it off him to the floor, and grabbed him into a full embrace, one in which Hynd was wracked with shaking shivers. She didn't let go until the shaking stopped.

Mac laughed from where he sat on the floor.

"Hell, if I knew it was that simple, I'd have stepped outside and get cold and wet myself."

Hynd extricated himself from Svetlanova's embrace and acknowledged her with little more than a nod before crouching to Mac's side.

"You got a fag, Mac? I'm gasping."

"You gave up five years ago."

"I figured now's as good a time as any to fall off the wagon. I won't tell my missus if you don't."

Mac lit cigarettes for all three of them.

"How's it going outside, Sarge?"

Hynd took a deep drag of his smoke before replying; hardly any came back out. If Svetlanova had tried it, she knew she'd be coughing for a week.

"We've got the drilling rig uncoupled but we're still sitting in the same place, tight up against it. The buggering anchor chains are a bastard to cut through. We're about halfway through the first of the two."

Svetlanova spoke first.

"The drilling rig is free standing in this storm? I thought for sure it would blow over if the cables were removed."

"Aye, we did too, lass," Hynd replied, taking another prodigious draw of smoke into his lungs. "But it's still there."

"Do we have enough juice to get the job done?" Mac asked.

Hynd didn't reply at first, then spoke softly.

"Maybe aye, maybe no," he said. "It'll be close."

Mac laughed.

"Maybe I'll get lucky and go first."

His bandages were soaked green again but he refused to let Svetlanova clean the wound this time.

"I heard you afore, lass, when you were talking to the cap. You shouldn't be touching the green shite. Leave it be. Most of it is inside me anyway, so leave it there where it is." He looked up at Hynd. "Just do me a favor, Sarge? Put me down before it gets too bad? I don't want to see myself melting into a wee puddle of green puke and pish. Promise me?"

Hynd took Mac's good hand.

"I'll see you right, lad. Don't worry about it. But hang on as long as you can. I think the wind's dropped a wee bit and the sleet has slackened. We might be out of this weather in time for the chopper to get to us yet. Just don't give up on me."

They gripped hands tightly and both had tears in their eyes when Hynd stood.

"It's bloody freezing out there," he said. "And here you are in here, sitting on your arse, smoking fags and getting attended to by a beautiful Russian spy. You lucky bastard."

"I am not a spy," Svetlanova said, then realized she was being made fun of.

"Let a dying man have one last wish," Mac said. "I always wanted to be James Bond."

"You don't have the tadger for it, man," Hynd said. "I've seen you in the showers."

"Hey, it's bloody cold. If you had any tackle in your trousers, you'd have noticed."

Svetlanova was still laughing when the door slammed open again and Banks returned.

"One chain down, one to go," he said as he came in and Hynd, barely warmed since his last stint, went back out into the storm.

- 17 -

When the Russian woman unzipped his parka, pulled it off, and hugged him hard, Banks didn't know whether to reciprocate or push her away.

"It's okay, Cap," Mac said from his seated position. "She's like that with all the lads. Except for me. She only likes me for my fags. How are we doing out there?"

"Touch and go," Banks replied. He was starting to get feeling back in his fingers now, a burning sensation like they were being run over a flame. He still had the flare of the cutter behind his eyelids when he closed the door, as if he'd looked too long at the sun, and a pounding headache made all his speech sound as if it came booming down a long dark tunnel. "We got through the first anchor chair and let it drop a few minutes ago. Did bugger all for our position though; the second chain is the one holding us tight in place. We've made a start on it but I doubt we've got enough juice left in the cylinders to finish the job. It's touch and go."

"Aye? Well, it's all chocolates and roses in here, as you can see. The sarge says the wind's dying down?"

"Aye, there's that at least. And the sleet's nearly stopped. Hold on, Mac. The chopper will be here before you know it."

"So everybody keeps telling me," Mac replied.

The Glaswegian didn't look well. The green veins pulsed strongly at his neck, his bandaged wrist had soaked through and dripped green goop on the deck and his face was gray, ashen, with a cold sweat pouring from his brow. But he still managed a smile when he looked up to Banks and Svetlanova.

"You can let go of him now, lass. He's a married man and his missus gets jealous quick."

Banks disengaged himself from the woman and checked his watch.

"Keep an eye on the corridor, Mac," he said. "I need to check in one last time."

Mac reached for his weapon and couldn't quite control it, until Svetlanova bent and made sure he had the rifle gripped, one-handed, pointing down the corridor. She crouched beside the seated man and lifted Nolan's weapon, sighting it on the same spot.

"Any time you're ready, Cap," she said in a perfect imitation of Mac's accent.

"We'll make a Scotswoman out of ye yet, lass," Mac said. "Would you like to meet ma auld maw? She'd love you."

Banks got the phone out of its pocket on the second try; his hands were still numb and tingling and his fingers felt too much like cold sausages but finally he got the number coded in and heard the ringing at the other end.

As he answered, he saw the Russian woman stiffen and caught a movement in the shadows along the corridor, something low, scuttling, headed their way.

"Check in," he said.

The voice surprised him at the other end by changing protocol.

"Check in. There will be a short delay in pick up due to adverse weather conditions in your area. Keep the package ready."

The line went dead, but he'd been on the call long enough to get the attention of one of the beasts. It came along the corridor fast, almost as wide as the distance the walls were apart, scampering and scratching, like a flattened barrel on legs.

Banks bent to reach his own weapon but his hands were still too numb and he fumbled, almost dropped the rifle. The beast kept coming but he needn't have worried. As if synchronized, Svetlanova and Mac fired simultaneously, three rounds each, tight into the thing's face. It dropped, flat on the floor now, some five yards from them and lay still.

"Give the lass a job, Cap," Mac said. "She's a natural."

*

"The chopper's definitely incoming," Banks said once his ears stopped ringing. "It all depends on when this bloody wind dies down."

"Should we get the sarge and McCally to stop cutting?"

"No. I still want away a bit from the rig in case any more of those big buggers come up."

"And how about the ones down in the cargo bay?"

"I'm wondering about that myself," Banks replied. "After we get on the chopper, we can get them to call in a strike. We could call it now but then we'd be fucked if the weather didn't improve."

"I'm fucked anyway, either way," Mac said and lit another cigarette for himself and Svetlanova. He went to hand hers over, then took it back and showed her the filter; it was tinged green where it had been at his lips.

"I ken you were looking forward to it but it looks like a last kiss is out of the question, lass," he said.

*

Banks went back out into the storm twice more; the second time he was with McCally when the oxy cylinder finally spluttered and gave up the ghost. They were only two-thirds of the way through the second anchor chain.

It wasn't enough.

"Fuck it. We've done all we can," he shouted to McCally. "It's the chopper or nothing now."

They went back inside to join the others. The sleet had stopped completely now and the wind had definitely moderated.

But has it moderated enough?

Come on, guys. Do us a solid here and get us off this fucking boat.

- 18 -

Talking was about all Mac had left to him but he had plenty of it. He'd kept up a series of anecdotes and remembrances the whole time the work was continuing out on the deck.

"I'm like a fucking librarian, me," he said, tapping at his forehead with his good hand. "I've got all the history of the squad up here. Every scrape we've got into and out of, who fucked up, who was a hero, all the times we saved each other or got saved. What's going to happen to all of that?"

Svetlanova was only half listening. Her gaze kept returning to the dead isopod in the corridor. As a scientist, she wanted to be studying it, learning its secrets. But as a human being, she wanted it gone, out of sight and out of mind, to a dark place where it could rot forever. She'd missed a question and Mac was looking at her, expecting an answer.

"Sorry," she said. "I'm wondering what happens to me, if we get out of here."

"I would nae worry, lass. You're not our first political prisoner. You're not even our first Russian. There'll be some questions in London, then retirement, and a wee pension somewhere in the country, if you want it."

She laughed.

"That's probably better than I'd get if I went back to Moscow."

Mac smiled, then coughed and wiped green-flecked spittle from his lips.

"I'd invite you to Glasgow for a sightseeing tour," he said. "But I think I'll be otherwise engaged, being dead and all."

She knew better than to attempt an answer. It was hard enough for him to keep his own fear at bay without dealing with hers too. The smell of rot came off him in waves now, an acrid stench that had to be fought down when it tickled at the back of the throat. Green ran in the big veins at his neck, his eyes were as red as hot coals, and now the veins at his cheeks showed green too.

If her experience with Nolan earlier was anything to go by, Mac didn't have long left to him. She didn't want to watch another die; the memories of the first were going to haunt her for the rest of her life. Two might be too much. When Banks and McCally came back in to report the attempt to remove the anchor had proved unsuccessful, she took the opportunity to step up the stairs and out onto the deck to smoke a cigarette on her own.

*

The storm had abated; the wind still came hard and strong from the north but there was no sleet and the dark clouds were already breaking up overhead, with a hint of blue showing in places the more north she looked toward the horizon. The boat listed slightly to starboard and the drilling rig swayed and creaked alarmingly.

But we're still afloat. And I'm not dead.

She cupped the cigarette in the bowl of her palm against the wind and tried to find a calm spot in the myriad of images and impressions flooding her mind. For the first time in days, she allowed hope to rise in her.

I might survive this.

Then she thought of the Glaswegian; a man who had shown her nothing but humor and kindness; a dying man.

He doesn't deserve to die alone.

She flicked the butt of the cigarette into the wind and turned to go back inside. That's when she heard it, far off and almost lost in the wind but distinctive enough it couldn't be misidentified, the *whop-whop* of a helicopter. She turned, trying to locate the source and saw it, a black dot in the west, approaching fast.

*

Captain Banks reacted swiftly to her news.

"Sarge, you bring Mac. Up onto the deck, right now. We want this to go by the numbers."

In less than a minute, they were all out on the deck, standing at the prow while the chopper came in from the west. It was obvious the pilot was fighting to maintain a straight line in the wind but the black dot got larger quickly. Svetlanova saw its lights, bright in the gloom under the still lowering clouds.

She stepped forward and took Banks' arm.

"Captain."

He turned and must have seen the concern in her face.

"What is it?"

She couldn't quite find the words to describe the fear suddenly leaping in her and opted for the simplest explanation she could muster.

"The chopper. It's all lit up."

"So what?"

"It's full of electricity."

*

"Shit. McCally, Sarge, get over to the gunwale and watch the drilling rig. If anything looks like coming up, put it back down hard and fast. I'll cover Mac when the chopper gets here. Once he and Svetlanova are on board, come back to me and we'll cover you."

The two men moved away to the side. Mac slumped, almost fell. His rifle clattered away on the deck and she saw he didn't have the energy left to retrieve it. Svetlanova put her shoulder under his good arm and held him up.

"Don't you fucking dare die on me, Mac," she said in his own accent. "Not when I'm on a promise to meet your maw."

If he replied she didn't hear him above the noise of the approaching chopper, but she felt the squeeze as he held her tighter.

The chopper hovered twenty feet above the deck and started a slow descent.

Svetlanova was beginning to believe she and Mac might get out of it alive when the attack came.

Nothing came up the rig but they'd been outflanked without even considering the possibility of it; the doors of the cargo hold burst open. An isopod the size of a truck burst out from almost immediately below the chopper and reached upward. One of its tentacles waved too close to the rotors. The tentacle was snipped off, almost cleanly but it had been strong enough to disrupt the blades and the chopper fell, heavily onto the deck, where it was immediately engulfed by a swarm of smaller isopods pouring up and out of the hold in a wave. The chopper slid sideward as the larger isopod pushed it across the deck; Svetlanova had to drag Mac aside to avoid them both being chopped to pieces by the tail rotor. The chopper crashed, headlong into the drilling rig which started to topple with the combined weight of chopper and isopods pressing against it.

Everything went over the side and down into the water; chopper, rig, and isopods in a squirming mass, all over the side and away into the deep. The boat shuddered, a collision somewhere below the water line that Svetlanova guessed must be part of the drilling rig hitting the hull.

The deck of the boat heaved and there was a crack, loud like thunder, as the anchor chain finally gave way and the boat lurched, rolling heavily to starboard. The prow rose, only to splash down hard again, sending water spraying all over the forward deck, soaking them all up to their thighs.

Then, suddenly, all was calm. Eerily quiet. Even the wind had died, holding its breath to see what happened next. The boat beneath them turned slowly with the wind and drifted slowly southward, heavy in the water.

Mac spoke, almost a whisper, in her ear.

"Well, that's us fucked good and proper then."

- 19 -

For Banks, it all happened in slow motion and it took a few seconds to sink in how much had changed in so little a time. He ran to the gunwale and looked over; somewhere, somewhere deep, a blue shimmering luminescence dropped away from them into the darkness. Everything left of the drilling rig went with it, including the broken canvas and wood remains of the kayaks they'd used to come aboard. There was no sign of the chopper, or its crew.

The anchor chain had finally given way at the weak spot where they'd been cutting but in being dragged overboard, it had torn a chunk of the keel away with it. There was also the fact the boat was limping along at the whim of the wind. At the moment, it looked like they were headed straight for the bay where the harbor and post office sat, but it would only take a slight change for them to be heading into open water.

And then we really would be totally fucked.

He looked across the deck to where the cargo bay doors lay open, bent, buckled, and spread-eagled. There was a black hole there he didn't want to look into.

But someone will have to. And it will have to be done soon.

He walked back over to what was left of his squad; he saw the same worry in their eyes he was sure must be in his own.

Get them moving. And do it fast, before they have too much time to think.

"Sarge, McCally, watch the bloody cargo bay. I need to call in a strike on this boat."

Svetlanova spoke first.

"Not the boat. The rig. Down there on the seabed, they're still coming through the hole we drilled. They'll keep coming through until the breach is shut. That's where the big ones are."

"Let them stay there," McCally said. "I want off this fucking boat."

"We can't," Svetlanova said. "They crawl. They travel in swarms on the seabed. Don't you see? How do you think those ones you met first got ashore?" She turned back to Banks. "If you're calling in a strike, make it a big one and make it on the rig, what's left of it, down on the bottom."

"Listen to the lass, Cap," Mac said weakly. "She kens what she's on about."

Banks nodded. He'd already made his mind up anyway.

"As I said. Watch the cargo bay, lads. I'll call in the strike."

He got the phone out of his pocket and punched in the code.

"Pick up aborted catastrophically," he said. "Calling for wildfire, at this location, ASAP."

"How big do you need?"

"Everything you've got," Banks said.

"Bad?"

"As bad as it gets."

"Wilco," the voice at the other end replied. "Wildfire in one hour from this mark. Good luck."

Banks looked at his squad.

"You heard? We've got incoming."

"How do we get off the boat?" McCally asked as Banks put the phone away. He still had his weapon trained on the cargo bay but, thankfully, there had been no movement from the darkness below.

"We don't. Not yet," Banks replied. "If the boat's going to hit the shore, we need to clear it of those bloody isopods first. If we're lucky, they all buggered off with the big one chasing the chopper. But we need to check.

"We've got an hour."

*

"Good luck, Cap," Mac said. "But there'll be no running about in the dark for me. I'm done in here."

He slumped at Svetlanova's side and his legs went from under him. Hynd was at his side in a second and between the sarge and the woman, they got Mac back inside to where he'd been sitting earlier, at the foot of the steps inside the door to the deck.

He looked up and managed a wan smile.

"I think I'll sit here for a while, see what happens."

"I'll stay with him," Hynd said.

"No," Banks replied, feeling like a shit but knowing he was right to make the call. "I need you and McCally with me if we're to clear these vermin out."

"Then I'll stay with him," Svetlanova said.

Banks really needed to keep the woman close; she was the mission now, all that was left of it. But he couldn't leave Mac to die alone; not after he'd already left Nolan to the same fate earlier.

"Okay; keep the weapon," he said to Svetlanova. "And come and find us when you can."

He turned to Mac.

"Look after her, big man. Like you said afore, she's a keeper."

"Aye," Mac said. "My maw is going to be so pleased to meet her." He spoke again as Banks turned to leave. "And Cap... waste those fuckers. Waste them all."

*

Banks let McCally and Hynd have a last word with Mac. He moved away along the corridor, standing over the dead isopod that almost filled the walk space. It had leaked stinking green goop again on the floor and he took care not to stand in it. As he remembered the shots that killed it, he realized he knew something else: he had a surefire way of finding out if there were any beasts still on board. All he had to do was turn on the phone and they'd come running.

A plan started to form but he wasn't sure he liked it.

We're going to need more firepower.

- 20 -

Svetlanova watched the three men walk away until they were lost in the gloom farther down the corridor. She couldn't see that far quite as well as before but this wasn't more cloud cover coming over.

It's getting dark again already.

Mac tried to get a cigarette from his packet but even that was too much of an effort for him. Green spittle flecked his lips and his eyes weren't red now but milky – opaque, with a hint of green.

"Are you still there, lass?" he said softly. "It's getting awful dark in here."

"I'm here, Mac," she replied and took his good hand in both of hers. It felt cold, clammy – a dead man's hand.

"I'm damned sorry you have to see me like this," he said. "But I don't want you fretting after I'm gone. This is the life I chose; it was always going to end in some deserted boat, or a road in the desert, or an empty power station. I was always going to be somewhere I wasn't supposed to be. Same as it ever was for me, ask my maw when you see her."

"I will," she said and knew she meant it. "I promise."

She lit a cigarette for them both and put one gently between his lips, where he puffed on it feebly.

"Last one," he said. "Something else that will please maw."

They smoked in silence, Mac enjoying the cigarette, Svetlanova because she had no clue what she might say to help in any way to ease what was imminent. Mac smoked his cigarette all the way down to the butt, then spat it out, leaving Svetlanova to grind it out with her heel.

"That's that then, lass," he said. "Time to go."

He pulled away from her grip and reached, fumbling blindly for his weapon.

"No!" Svetlanova said and knocked his hand away from the

weapon.

"Yes," he replied softly and reached for the gun again. "I told you earlier. I don't want to go like Nolan. I'm a soldier. Let me die like one."

She helped him find the rifle and put it in his hand but he couldn't grip it; all the strength had gone from him.

"I'll need a bit of help here, lass," he said. He coughed and watery green fluid flecked with blood ran over his chin. "Quickly now. Please? It's getting really fucking dark in here."

She helped him get the weapon under his chin.

"Tell my maw I always loved her," he said. "And give her a kiss from me."

They both had fingers on the trigger but Svetlanova was the one who pulled it, sending two rounds into Mac's head. He slumped aside, leaving a smear on the wall where he'd rested.

It was mainly green.

Svetlanova rose, tears blinding her, hefted a rifle in her arms and headed off, not really caring where she was going, needing to put as much space as she could for now between herself and the body of her dead friend.

- 21 -

Two quick shots echoed around Banks, McCally, and Hynd as they approached the stern. All three stopped to listen. If there were more shots, it meant a firefight and they'd go to the aid of whoever was shooting. But all fell quiet again.

"Mac?" McCally said and Hynd nodded.

"I think so."

"Bugger."

Banks looked at the other two.

"Nobody else gets dead here. Are we clear? We're all walking out of this. We owe them that much."

"I hear you, Cap," Hynd said. "But we're not having much luck this time around. A strike's incoming and we're adrift, dead in the water. Do we have a plan?"

"I'm working on it," Banks said. He tapped at the phone. "We can bring these fuckers to us anytime we want with this. But we don't have enough firepower between the three of us to hold back a swarm. We need more bang for our buck."

"Well, unless we're leaking fuel – and I didn't see any sign of it on the way in – a boat this size carries a lot of diesel," McCally said.

"Aye. And it's somewhere in yon freezing, flooded, engine room," Banks replied. "I'd already thought of that. But in her story, Svetlanova mentioned they also carried kerosene; lots of it. Anybody seen it?"

The other two shook their heads.

"But there's plenty of places we haven't been."

"Aye," Banks replied. "And barely enough time to search. But let's get to it. It's double time from here on, lads. And if we don't drift far enough, the strike's going to take us out along with everything else in a wide area, so don't even bother worrying yet."

*

They searched from the stern forward, moving quickly. They didn't find kerosene, or much of anything worthwhile in the crew quarters and engineer's workroom that had been swept earlier. Their luck changed at the lifeboats, where Hynd came up with a small box of six emergency flares he removed from the box and stowed in his webbing belt as they went back inside and then quickly through the rest of the decks.

They still didn't find kerosene but they did find Svetlanova, standing in the open doorway of the big pantry, eating hard biscuits, tears still running down her face.

"Mac's dead?" McCally asked.

Svetlanova only nodded, tears running down her face.

"You were with him at the end?" Banks asked her.

She nodded again but still didn't speak, just kept eating, almost mechanically. He squeezed past her, into the pantry and immediately saw what he should have also considered earlier. He kicked at a row of a dozen or so ten-liter containers on the floor.

"Well, there's no kerosene," he called out. "But there's plenty of cooking oil, gallons of it. Enough to get a job done. Now we need somewhere to stand."

*

"We didn't check the cargo hold for yon beasties, Cap," McCally said.

"Aye. That was deliberate. If the fuckers are in there, I didn't want to disturb them before we had the weapons we needed for a fight. You saw how they came up out of there when the chopper came; we could try to take them again on the forward deck, although we'd be wide open if there's a lot of them. Or we could go high, up on the top of the superstructure again. I'm swithering between the two of them."

"If I get a vote, I say go high," Hynd replied. "If there's any more of those bigger fuckers still around, I want to see them coming."

"I'm with the sarge," McCally chipped in.

Svetlanova still said nothing. She had Nolan's rifle slung over her shoulder and Banks considered taking it from her but decided to let her be; she was in shock, clearly. But she'd also proved she could handle herself in a clinch – at least he hoped so, for they were surely going to need her on a gun before this was over.

"The top deck it is then," he said. "Sarge, you take Svetlanova and half of this oil; get it up on top. McCally, you're with me with the rest of it."

*

It took three trips to get six canisters of oil up onto the top deck. On the second trip, Banks had looked up to see Hynd giving him an okay sign from the top deck. It was getting dark now, the last rays of the sun washing the sea and horizon way off to the west. They were drifting, slowly, southward with the wind and the dark bulk of the island was straight ahead of them, still several hundred yards distant but getting closer. Banks tried to gauge the distance they'd traveled and how much they still had to go if they wanted to escape the coming air strike.

He saw McCally look at the island, then at him.

"It's going to be touch and go, isn't it, Cap?"

Banks nodded.

"And if the tide turns against us, it's not going to end well. Let's get this oil poured. We've got work to do."

*

They poured oil until all six containers were empty, concentrating on the area between the open cargo bay doors and the superstructure. The list of the boat meant the heavy oil started to run but it was mostly running toward the open hold, so Banks let it find its own level. With the last canister, he got close to the dark opening. He chanced a look down. It was almost black down there but he heard them, skittering and scratching and saw faint but definite movement; blue and shimmering.

I see you, you wee buggers.

He saw no sign of anything larger than the dog-sized ones.

But it doesn't mean there aren't any there. It's a big hold.

He looked up to see McCally empty the last of his oil close to where the deck met the superstructure. He jerked his thumb upward.

It was almost show time. He had one last thing to attend to; he led McCally to the stern and had him help while they readied one of the lifeboats so it could be released quickly from its cradle.

"The bloody thing's holed, Cap," McCally said.

"Aye, lad. I'm not blind. But if I'm right, it won't need to take us far; and it might be the thing that gets us out of here in one piece."

And now it is show time.

- 22 -

"Are you okay?" Hynd asked Svetlanova as they each carried the last two canisters of cooking oil up from the larder to the top deck. Her arms hurt from the two previous journeys, she felt dog tired and ready to lie down and sleep. But it wasn't what the sergeant was asking her and they both knew it.

"I'll live," she replied, then realized in her tiredness she'd spoken in Russian, so she repeated it in English. "I'll live. It's seeing them go so fast; it's not something I'm going to forget in a while."

Hynd hefted his two oil canisters up onto the top deck, then came back down to take hers.

"We remember them," he said. "In our thoughts, in our stories, in our dreams, and in the dark nights when we can't sleep."

"We're their libraries, as they were ours? Is that it?"

"Aye, lass. You talked to Mac long enough to learn that, at least. He'd have liked that."

He lifted the canisters up top, then came back to lend her a hand up the short steps to the upper deck.

It was almost full dark now, only the last glimmer of sunlight far to the west. A crescent moon rose in the east and the sky had cleared from the north, with a blanket of stars slowly taking form overhead. She'd always loved nights like this in the past and had stood on the deck for long hours, marveling at the sky until the cold forced her inside for bonhomie and chatter with the kitchen crew, then vodka and chess with the captain.

All gone now, never to return.

Now the boat felt as dead as the empty place in her heart. She pulled her jacket closed and put up her hood against the cold. She had thick, fur-lined gloves in her pockets but kept her hands uncovered for now; the metal of the weapon already felt icy cold in her hands but she wouldn't be able to pull the trigger if gloved.

And I've got a feeling the shooting is going to start soon.

She looked ahead; the boat was pointed, straight as an arrow, at the island ahead and the wind was still at their back, although nowhere near as strong as it had been an hour before. But they didn't seem to be getting any closer to land and the boat felt heavy and sluggish, without its usual slow yaw; now it was more of a floundering, like a dog paddling frantically trying to keep afloat rather than the smooth stroke of a seasoned swimmer.

*

Captain Banks and McCally climbed up through the hatchway a few minutes later.

"Make sure you've got a full mag to start with," Banks said. "This is going to go fast and hot. And if you have to reload, step back behind the others, let them cover you."

He was speaking for her benefit and she nodded to show she understood. She had to ask for a spare magazine from McCally.

"How are we doing for ammo, Sarge?" Banks asked.

They did a check. Both the sarge and Banks had three mags each. McCally had two and Svetlanova had the fresh one she'd been given and six rounds left in the one she replaced.

"So there's that," the sarge said when they were done, "these flares I got from the lifeboat, and these bottles of oil here. Not a lot."

"But it'll have to be enough. It's all we've got. When I say run, you run, all of you, no heroes. Either down the stairs or down the hatch; take the quickest route for you and meet at the port side lifeboat; the shackles are loosened so we can get it in the water fast. Remember, nobody else dies here."

Banks took out the satellite phone and switched it on.

Down in the cargo bay, the blue luminescence shifted.

- 23 -

The small isopods emerged first, scuttling over the rim of the hold, scores of them, all moving with a single purpose, heading for the superstructure.

"Don't shoot," Banks said. He dropped the phone, still switched on, into his inside pocket. "We want as many of the buggers up here where we can see them as possible."

The dog-sized isopods kept pouring out of the hold and across the forward deck. Hynd and McCally moved to join Banks on his left and Svetlanova stepped up on his right so all four were in a line looking down over the length of the boat. Banks realized they hadn't given Svetlanova a pair of night glasses but it hardly mattered; the blue luminescence coming off the isopods lent the whole scene an eerie glow more than bright enough to see by.

The only sound was the clickity-clack of talons on deck as the isopods came forward toward them. Banks shoved his earplugs deep in both ears and saw Svetlanova had torn up a bandage and was stuffing them in as makeshift plugs of her own. She finished and gave him an 'OK' sign. He realized he knew nothing of the woman's past before her time on the boat but he wouldn't be surprised to find she had military training; she handled herself as confidently as most men he'd served with and a damn sight better than some. He knew he wouldn't have to watch out for her in the imminent firefight.

Which is just as well. I think we're going to be busy.

*

The first of the smaller isopods reached the bottom of the superstructure and started to climb. Banks hefted one of the canisters of oil.

"One each, pour it down over them, quickly now."

Everybody moved to comply and they send a wash of oil down the side and over the approaching swarm. It didn't slow them any, although the blue shimmer took on a rainbow aurora at the foot of the superstructure that might have been almost beautiful in different circumstances.

"Sarge, give me two of those flares. Hold onto yours until I say otherwise."

Hynd moved quickly to comply, then all four of them lined up, rifles poised, watching the swarming beasts scuttle up the side toward them. They weren't finding it easy; the gasoline had made the surface slippery and they went backward almost as much as they came forward but they were piling up, force of numbers and pressure from below allowing them to gain height. The nearest of them was now almost halfway up.

"Cap?" McCally said.

"Not yet," Banks replied.

The head of the swarm was almost two-thirds of the way up when Banks saw what he'd been waiting for; two of the larger, pickup truck-sized isopods scuttled up out of the dark hold, heading for the superstructure. He waited to see if more were going to appear but they were the last things to come up out of the dark.

I can only hope that's all of them.

"Fire at will," he shouted and the night air filled with the roar of gunfire.

*

At first, they targeted their fire on the swarm of smaller isopods on the superstructure, sending the front rows of them down and back into the others, where a feeding frenzy commenced, making more of them easy targets. But there were others who were still concerned with climbing and they came on fast.

And they ate bullets; if the aim wasn't accurate enough, a shot into the body rather than the face did little to slow them. Despite their volley fire, the beasts kept getting higher.

Banks' first magazine was running low. Instead of stepping

back to reload, he shouted.

"Fire in the hold," he said and pulled the string of a flare, dropping it over the side before it blazed in his face.

An orange glow lit up the whole forward deck, then the flare hit the isopods and the swarm around the superstructure went up with a whoosh and a searing wall of flame that almost reached the four defenders on the top deck, forcing them to step back and turn away from the heat.

Banks slammed in a fresh mag, counted to ten, and watched the orange glow subside slightly then turned again to the rail. The other three joined him and once again they poured round after round down into what was now a much-reduced swarm, some of which burned even as they kept trying to climb.

The two large isopods had kept back from the fray so far but they now moved forward toward the base of the superstructure, drawn, as Banks had hoped, by the easy scavenging to be had on the dead.

He stopped firing and poured the last two canisters of oil down over the side. It hit the isopods and immediately started to burn, catching both the larger ones and sending them scurrying back. He lit the second flare and threw it over the top of all the isopods, to the oil-soaked deck behind them.

"Time to go," he shouted, as the flare blazed like a miniature sun and the whole forward deck went up in a sheet of flame. The isopods danced in fire.

- 24 -

Svetlanova reached the top of the stairs first and led others down. A hellish orange glow lit the steps and the cold of the night air was punctuated with washes of heat, almost burning hot. She swept the light of the rifle ahead of her, checking the darker shadows at the corners, ready to shoot at the slightest provocation.

None came and she reached the rear deck without anything coming at her. McCally came down next beside her and together they made their way quickly to the port side lifeboat. Svetlanova started to step up to the lowering mechanism.

"I've got this," McCally said. "You check the body of the boat. Get in if it's all clear. We're going to be leaving in a hurry."

Hynd arrived next and Svetlanova, with the sarge's help, pulled off the canvas sheet from the boat while McCally covered them; the bottom of the lifeboat was empty of isopods but the holed hull was clearly visible. Hynd balled up the canvas sheet and held it over the hole but it obviously wasn't big enough to use as a plug.

"Jackets," he shouted and all three of them shucked off their outer garment. Hynd bundled them, along with the canvas sheet, into a firm ball he kicked, hard, into the hole.

"It won't last long," he said.

Banks arrived and joined McCally at the side of the boat.

"It won't have to. Get the outboard going, Sarge, if you can. If not, McCally, you and I are on the oars. Svetlanova, you get to watch the plug. See if you can find something to use to bail with; I've got a feeling we're going to need it."

*

Svetlanova rummaged in the small compartment at the prow of the boat and found a mop and a small bucket but nothing else of use. The bucket would have to do. She heard the thrum and felt a vibration as the outboard kicked in.

"Drop it," Banks shouted.

At the same time, one of the large isopods barreled down the superstructure stairs, trailing fire. McCally and Banks didn't hesitate; they emptied their mags into it, then had to jump as the lifeboat tumbled out into empty air. The isopod reached for them, with limbs that looked like arms of fire.

The men landed hard but now both Svetlanova and Hynd had stood, taken aim, and aimed another volley at the beast. It hung on the edge of the deck for a long second then fell forward, hitting the water a second after the boat did. It sank with the hiss of extinguishing flame, then was gone behind them as the motor bit in the water and they surged forward.

The bung Hynd had shoved into the hole started to come loose almost immediately, water pouring in at the edges of the hole. Svetlanova had time for one look toward the dark shadow marking the harbor, far too far away, then had to deploy the bucket.

Hynd came beside her and used the mop to try to keep the bung in place. It helped but not much. She noticed as she bailed there was a sheen, oily and thick, on the water she was bailing and she smelled it as she threw a bucketful overboard; diesel.

The bottom of the lifeboat filled faster, much faster, than she could bail.

- 25 -

Banks struggled with the tiller, trying to keep the lifeboat in a straight line and heading for the harbor. The vessel wallowed heavy in the water and every so often the outboard propeller would hit a chunk of thicker slush or ice and the whole frame would lurch and shudder, the prow splashing hard in seas high in a swell from the previous storm. McCally stood beside him, looking back at the boat they'd abandoned.

"The fires are out, Cap. And I can't see any beasties."

"Well, there's that to be thankful for anyway."

In front of him in the lifeboat, Svetlanova and Hynd tried to keep the influx of water to a minimum but Banks knew it was a losing battle; cold water already pooled at his feet and he felt the ice bite through his boots. He pulled down his night vision glasses and looked over the bailers' heads to the shore beyond. They were definitely closing, even as the abandoned cargo boat behind them kept coming at their rear, a slow, painfully slow race to the small dock at the settlement's harbor.

The water grew even choppier as they got closer to shore. White-topped waves crashed against the pebbles ahead; he heard the rattle of them, even above the outboard. The tiller bucked in his hand, threatening to tear out of his grasp. The fight against the influx of water wasn't going well either and icy slush lapped almost up to Bank's ankles. The weight of water in the bottom of the lifeboat helped to stabilize it somewhat but it was cancelled out by the fact they were now definitely sinking. Banks turned the engine to full throttle, aimed it straight at the rocky shore and prayed.

*

They hit the bottom five yards from shore with a shudder,

tearing the outboard off the back and threatening to tip them all over completely. A wave caught them and moved them a yard closer, then threatened to suck them back out again as it receded.

"All ashore who are going ashore," Banks shouted and then was out of the boat and wading thigh deep in freezing cold sea, making his balls shrink and his legs turn to stone that had to be forced into movement for every inch to be made toward dry land. Another wave hit, almost knocking him over, then the backwash tugged hard at him. By the time he hauled himself up the small slope, fighting the surge and wash of pebbles underfoot, he felt like he'd run five miles in full gear.

The other three hauled themselves out to join him. They all looked to be as soaked and exhausted as he felt but he knew they couldn't afford to stand still; they'd be dead in minutes.

"Keep moving," he said. "We need to get to shelter and try to get some heat into us. Double time, head up to yon house with the big garage."

He turned to start running but McCally shouted as his back.

"We've got problems, Cap."

He turned to look. The huge black keel of the cargo boat loomed offshore, the tear at the water line clearly visible, made prominent by the fact blue luminescence shimmered all around it, a blue quickly spreading into the surrounding waters. Far from killing all the beasts, it looked like all they'd succeeded in doing was stirring more into action.

*

"Get off the shore," Banks shouted. "Maybe they won't be interested in us."

They retreated, fighting the loose pebbles, climbing up the short incline to the shore track, then back farther, quickly past the burned-out remains at the harbor.

Banks risked a look back as they reached the driveway of the large house; the beasts were already swarming again, pouring out of the keel and into the water. Up on the deck of the cargo boat that now dominated the small harbor, a new blue aurora swelled and grew. Something came up and out of the hold; something bigger than anything they'd seen so far; an isopod so tall its head reached the top deck of the superstructure. It shimmered blue along its whole length and smaller pieces of blue fell off it in droves; pieces scurrying and skittering all over the deck where they landed.

It's giving birth.

"They're still coming, Cap," McCally said.

A horde of isopods washed off the deck and into the water, filling the harbor area, a blue carpet clambering over each other on their haste to get at them.

"Shit," Banks muttered. "The phone. I forgot to switch off the bloody phone."

- 26 -

Svetlanova heard the captain mutter and saw him fumble, hands too cold for the task, at his jacket, trying to get at the inside pocket.

She remembered the burnings; the ship's captain pouring kerosene down the rig, the other captain lighting the oil on the deck, and the red glare of the blazing flare.

She turned to Hynd and, before the sarge had time to complain, pulled one of the flares from his webbing belt.

"The water. It's full of diesel," she said, already turning away and pulling the string on the flare.

She ran forward three steps and threw it, a high and handsome arc toward the harbor. Hynd had seen her plan immediately and a second flare blazed only two seconds after hers, both of them falling into the harbor, right among the shimmering blue.

"Everybody down," Hynd shouted and pushed Svetlanova to the ground, lying almost on top of her. She was only able to turn her head but it was enough to see the result.

The harbor went up first, a wall of orange flame flash-frying the isopods and eating them away even as it sped across the open sea and took hold around the rent in the cargo ship's hull. The huge isopod on the deck screamed as the small ones burned and popped, then it too took hold, fire washing up and around the superstructure.

The whole boat went up with a muffled crump. A wave of heat blew across the harbor as the boat collapsed in on itself and the isopods burned.

*

It was some time before Hynd moved to let her stand.

The cargo boat still burned outside the harbor but the seas around were now dark, with no sign of any blue shimmer.

Banks stood above them as they got up, with the phone in his hand.

"It's still on. If there's any of them left, we'll know soon enough."

They waited for minutes but there was only the burning boat.

"Good enough," Banks said. "Let's get some shelter before we freeze our bollocks off."

*

They were inside the large house, with a propane heater going full blast, when they heard the sound of approaching aircraft. They watched from the porch as two bomb runs passed over where the rig had been and the water rose each time in a huge bubble of foaming water. There was no sign of any blue.

"Will it be enough?" Banks asked.

Svetlanova replied how she thought Mac might have wanted her to, in her best Glaswegian accent.

"Fucked if I know, Cap," she said.

CHECK OUT OTHER GREAT HORROR NOVELS

BLACK FRIDAY
by Michael Hodges

Jared the kleptomaniac, Chike the unemployed IT guy, Patricia the shopaholic, and Jeff the meth dealer are trapped inside a Chicago supermall on Black Friday. Bridgefield Mall empties during a fire alarm, and most of the shoppers drive off into a strange mist surrounding the mall parking lot. They never return. Chike and his group try calling friends and family, but their smart phones won't work, not even Twitter. As the mist creeps closer, the mall lights flicker and surge. Bulbs shatter and spray glass into the air. Unsettling noises are heard from within the mist, as the meth dealer becomes unhinged and hunts the group within the mall. Cornered by the mist, and hunted from within, Chike and the survivors must fight for their lives while solving the mystery of what happened to Bridgefield Mall. Sometimes, a good sale just isn't worth it

GRIMWEAVE
by Tim Curran

In the deepest, darkest jungles of Indochina, an ancient evil is waiting in a forgotten, primeval valley. It is patient, monstrous, and bloodthirsty. Perfectly adapted to its hot, steaming environment, it strikes silent and stealthy, it chosen prey: human. Now Michael Spiers, a Marine sniper, the only survivor of a previous encounter with the beast, is going after it again. Against his better judgement, he is made part of a Marine Force Recon team that will hunt it down and destroy it.

The hunters are about to become the hunted.

CHECK OUT OTHER GREAT HORROR NOVELS

DEATH CRAWLERS
by Gerry Griffiths

Worldwide, there are thought to be 8,000 species of centipede, of which, only 3,000 have been scientifically recorded. The venom of Scolopendra gigantea—the largest of the arthropod genus found in the Amazon rainforest—is so potent that it is fatal to small animals and toxic to humans. But when a cargo plane departs the Amazon region and crashes inside a national park in the United States, much larger and deadlier creatures escape the wreckage to roam wild, reproducing at an astounding rate. Entomologist, Frank Travis solicits small town sheriff Wanda Rafferty's help and together they investigate the crash site. But as a rash of gruesome deaths befalls the townsfolk of Prospect, Frank and Wanda will soon discover how vicious and cunning these new breed of predators can be. Meanwhile, Jake and Nora Carver, and another backpacking couple, are venturing up into the mountainous terrain of the park. If only they knew their fun-filled weekend is about to become a living nightmare.

THE PULLER
by Michael Hodges

Matt Kearns has two choices: fight or hide. The creature in the orchard took the rest. Three days ago, he arrived at his favorite place in the world, a remote shack in Michigan's Upper Peninsula. The plan was to mourn his father's death and figure out his life. Now he's fighting for it. An invisible creature has him trapped. Every time Matt tries to flee, he's dragged backwards by an unseen force. Alone and with no hope of rescue, Matt must escape the Puller's reach. But how do you free yourself from something you cannot see?

**SEVERED**PRESS

 facebook.com/severedpress
 twitter.com/severedpress

CHECK OUT OTHER GREAT HORROR NOVELS

MONSTROSITY
by **Tim Curran**

The Food. It seeped from the ground, a living, gushing, teratogenic nightmare. It contaminated anything that ate it, causing nature to run wild with horrible mutations, creating massive monstrosities that roam the land destroying towns and cities, feeding on livestock and human beings and one another. Now Frank Bowman, an ordinary farmer with no military skills, must get his children to safety. And that will mean a trip through the contaminated zone of monsters, madmen, and The Food itself. Only a fool would attempt it. Or a man with a mission.

THE SQUIRMING
by **Jack Hamlyn**

You are their hosts

You are their food

The parasites came out of nowhere, squirming horrors that enslaved the human race. They turned the population into mindless pack animals, psychotic cannibalistic hordes whose only purpose was to feed them.

Now with the human race teetering at the edge of extinction, extermination teams are fighting back, killing off the parasites and their voracious hosts. Taking them out one by one in violent, bloody encounters.

The future of mankind is at stake.

And time is running out.

Made in the USA
Lexington, KY
18 April 2018